THE RAT
AND
THE ROSE

A NAUGHTOBIOGRAPHY

BY ARNOLD RABIN

BLACK•HERON•PRESS
Post Office Box 95676
Seattle, Washington 98145

PUBLISHED BY:
Black Heron Press
Post Office Box 95676
Seattle, Washington 98145

ISBN 0-930773-42-X (cloth)
ISBN 0-930773-43-8 (paper)

COVER ART BY:
Phillip Brazeau

PRODUCTION AND BOOK DESIGN BY:
Dataprose Typesetting, Seattle, Washington

Printed in Canada

For Sydell and David
who could find no other way
into this book . . .

ACKNOWLEDGMENTS

To the gods: the record stands!
To the National Endowment for the Arts: my thanks!

The plural of tooth is teeth;
Is the plural of booth then beeth?
The plural of mouse is mice;
Is the plural of spouse then spice?
The plural of that is those;
Is the plural of hat then hose,
And the plural of rat then rose?

Who knows?

– Author Unknown

PART ONE

The Charm's Wound Up

CHAPTER ONE
Demons Aroused

Oh, I turn away, even now as I begin! But there is little time left to me. And I know I must not hesitate! I must be unsparing with myself! Unfalteringly I must approach those involuted and thoroughly odious aspects of my being with unadulterated — how the word causes me to tremble, Emilia! — frankness! Indeed, I must penetrate and probe microcosmically, even macro-cosmically, the "deep well" of my unconscious! Nestling tarantella!

But I am not wholly to blame! No one life is made up only of its own evil! It is atrociously mutilated by the muddied meddlings of others. And I shall tell of them also, the many who have touched me, mauled me physically and spiritually: I shall spare no one — not even the wizened old lady who, spilling my glass of milk as she sat opposite me in the cafeteria, said, "God bless you, my boy! I too was a whore once." For all who have touched me are a part of me as I, appallingly enough, am a part of them, as they and I are a part of everyman, as which of us is not! We are one of us — all of us — and they too shall suffer! It is quite apparent!

Except Aunt Carole! Willow that she was, she stood apart from all of us! How else can I describe her! She was not fair of face nor baldly grotesque, but she exuded, because of this very nondescript appearance, that substantial comfort so cavalierly identified with the *demi-monde*. Yet, even this of her attributes was unimportant. It was her *vivo con brio* that enabled her to achieve supreme moments of elevation!

For example, on rainy days Aunt Carole would wash her hair — so modest, so commonplace an act, but then she would glorify this simple act by racing with cheetah grace throughout the house, her wet tresses lashing about her neck and face, her nude body prickled by goose-flesh and pimpled with those delicious droplets of water. And, like one of God's angels in heaven hallooing to a brother in Hell, she would implore, "Rain, Rain, go away, come again some other day!" These were the moments when I adored her with compassion and desire, when, with my child's arms, bone thin from the malnutrition brought on by my protest fasts, I could have crushed her to me. Guiltily, I say no overt act of a physically sexual nature ever occurred between us, for by so abstaining, I deprived myself and her of undue abundance. To be rewarded for my abstinence everlastingly by niggling frustration, demeaning to both our grandeurs!

But it was Aunt Carole's otherwise scrupulous passion for honesty that led to her undoing. And it is with the most violent of "emotion[s] recollected in tranquillity" that I relate the episode!

For my fifth birthday I received from Cousin Winthrop Adams an Indian headdress — large with furiously colored feathers stuck into an equally

furiously colored headband of cheap cheap calico. Its
blatant imitation, its unabashed fakery disgusted both
Aunt Carole and me. What had this to do with a child's
imagination which it had been designed to excite!
Instantly we understood one another! It had to be
destroyed! Without hesitation, but with those character-
istically savage movements of her head, Aunt Carole
traced the figure eight in the air and ran from the room,
returning a moment later with a dried branch and two
flint stones, for Aunt Carole scorned matches — too far
were they from the Sacred Promethean fire!

"Come child, we will burn it!" she sang. Then,
thinking better of her words, she altered her decision.
"No, it is not we who must burn it! It is thee who must
do it, thee thyself, and, in so doing, it is thee who will
have identified what is false and destroyed it!"

She held the headdress by its tail and, gazing at me,
her eyes wild with purpose, she cried out, "Rub the
stones and light the fire! Cleanse the earth of its
sandimonatheisomes!" Caught up with the significance
of my task, I rubbed the stones. Nothing happened. "Rub
again — and again — Don't ever give up! It is only when
thou givest up that thou truly loseth!" I rubbed again —
and again. The tiny bit of fire sparked, the feathers
flamed, and Aunt Carole, swirling the torch above her
head, finally flung the flagrant lie out the window,
exultantly hallooing like the devil in Hell to a brother in
Heaven, "Fire! Fire! Fire! Fire! Water! Water! Water!
Water! and, swinging me up into her arms, she held me

too out the window, pleading with sacrificial ardor, "Woodsman, spare the rod — oh, spare the rod and spoil the child!"

They took my Aunt Carole away — and a part of me went ALSO.

• • • • •

The part of me that stayed has become the me that people know as well as the me that people never know and the third me who is an amalgamation of the first and second, the fourth who scorns these three, and yet the fifth who pities the other four. And now the one part more which must look with dispassion of afterthought upon all the others! Even so!

While I am only too aware of the fragments I now am, I find myself nostalgically recalling that these same fragments were for one brief moment a single cell formed in the darkness of my mother's womb, when, in heat, my father — even he, "a beast that wants discourse of reason," — lay upon my mother, and satisfying his gross appetite, fell to rest upon her. At once the shattering conflict began! No matter how I tossed and turned, trying to repell him, he lingered! Helpless I was: no arms, no legs, no weapons to fight back with! Only a soul tormented, longing, but being brainless, as yet unable to devise a means to heave off this enormous burden. In the beginning, communication with my father was impossible. And so it has been ever since!

It was my mother who helped. Sensitive to my discomfort even then, she shifted her position. I, floating freely, must have gone to sleep. And, for a while I remember nothing.

• • • • •

Though I could be only a grave disappointment to my father who was constantly disappointed by whatever life offered him until he ultimately became a mushroom, I must admit to being also something of an unfortunate revelation to my mother. And more the irony of this since her maternal instinct had, from childhood, been strong, inordinately so, as evidence the fact that when she was twelve and a half, she tried to impregnate herself with the pollen of a rose, completely misinterpreting the biology of hybrids. Ten years later, upon my birth, she must still have anticipated that I might look something like a rose, an expectation which did irreparable harm to me since it resulted in her instantaneous rejection of me when I was first brought to her. Indeed, my initial remembrance of my mother is of her turning from me and plaintively uttering, "He looks like a rat!"

If this designation of my appearance as being rose-like or rat-like seems just an esoteric quibbling with imagery, I must explain it has profounder significance. I have suffered a distinct and at once elusive rose-rat complex, a dichotomy in my nature that is not merely a figment of my own over-stimulated imagination, but one

which you, dear reader, will soon agree was augment-
atively experienced. Yet, albeit the dislocating facts of
my life (and there were those who never knew the true
state of things), this duality was sensed by all who had
brush with me, dividing my acquaintances sharply into
two groups: those who found themselves inexplicably
and lovingly referring to me as Gregory the Rose, and
those, who, with equal intensity and similar
befuddlement as to their motives, preferred to think of
me as Gregory the Rat.

• • • • •

Now, as my candle burns lower, it is painful to
contemplate and analyze the events of those first few
hours of my life, but if I am to know my compleat man,
it is imperative that I do so. For, in those early hours,
certain recurrent responses were unalterably defined.
Despised by my father, rejected by my mother whose
initial reaction to me had been devastating, I felt equally
alone and rapidly consumed by a sense of inadequacy
which, feeding upon itself, logically and industriously
developed into undiluted self-hatred.

Yet, in everyman, waiting only to be touched is the
desire to love and be loved — agonizingly — as the guru
Miniharathomas, living in those select ridges of the
southernmost tip of Gilmartisa, told me. And even then
in those infant hours, as I lay *in extremis*, I knew there
was something larger to which I was entitled, a birthright

which is the legacy of every damned soul. And I rebelled at the first of life's deprivations. So acute was my indignation that when laid to suckle in my mother's arms, I nipped the breast that fed me, choosing rather to die of malnutrition than to survive on gall. My father, enraged at my impertinence, struck me. My mother, in an effort to compensate for the guilt which her own feelings towards me had aroused, struck my father. And the enduring pattern of our relationship was established.

The sadder all this in view of my mother's passionate yearning to love her first born! How cruel the fates! She could not even wholeheartedly reject my father's attitude because she was herself so distressed by my appearance; yet she realized she must disguise her feelings so that my father's negativism would not be intensified. For, if my father became aware of my mother's disappointment in me, he would have no reason to contain his urgings, and it remained within the realm of perfect possibility that he would murder me. It was only because my father depended so totally upon my mother, being rendered absolutely impotent (both figuratively and physically) when he incurred her disfavor, that he chose to tolerate my birth at all. So conscious was he of this dependency and so afraid of severing the bond which sustained him that he used every artifice to divert my mother from detecting his displeasure, managing besides to increase his attentions to her despite the fact that during her pregnancy she had grown fat, a physical state which, as might be expected, did nothing to alleviate her own annoyance with me whom, of course, she held responsible.

But my mother was not to be fooled by my father. She knew only too well that my father was not fundamentally an affectionate man, and that, if anything, his romantic inclinations towards her would have deteriorated with my birth. And while she was not above duplicity herself, she was repelled by a duplicity encouraged by such weakness, and she found it increasingly difficult to maintain any semblance of devotion for my father. Yet again she was helpless! For if she did not pretend to respond to what was not there in him to begin with, he would certainly detect her withdrawal of even the charity of pretense; and, believing it was caused by his own rejection of me, he might find this, too, reason for doing away with me. Either by revealing her true feelings towards me or by revealing her true feelings towards my father, my mother risked bringing about my annihilation.

Out of these subtle anxieties, there was one immediate positive outcome: my mother, whose emotions are easily triggered, was so wracked by her dilemma that her weight dropped; and, upon leaving the hospital, she found herself more svelte and attractive than ever before. It was with joy in my heart and hope everlasting that I heard her — all a-flutter and a-blush — promise the young doctor who discharged her, that if, in the near future, the Good Lord did see fit to take my father from her, she would, most assuredly, consider his now adulterous proposals.

CHAPTER TWO

The Origin of My Species

My ancestors are apparently few in number, since I can trace them back no further than my grandparents and even here, there are conflicting records. All the evidence at hand would seem to indicate that my father's father was not of woman born since he was found in a den of lions, just north of the little village of Tamburackoo on the west coast of Mirambella by the missionary's wife who became my paternal grandmother. From what I was able to learn from the ancient toothless one, Gurachievma, on my only visit to Mirambella, my grandfather lived with Lupercalia (for that was my paternal grandmother's Christian name) out of wedlock after expediently throwing her missionary husband to be devoured by that pride of lions among whom he himself had been raised. Lupercalia, whose background is completely obscured since her family had deserted her when she had chosen to walk through life with a minister of God, now devoted herself to trying to convert and train my grandfather who was, as might be expected, more lion than man. Astoundingly enough she did succeed in leading him through a mock marriage just before my father was born.

However, with my father's birth, my grandfather rejected any further training and spent most of his time sitting morosely on his haunches in the darkest corner of the cave. Lupercalia could no longer even prevail upon him to gather her food. And then one night she found him, looking more man than beast, holding the back of my father's neck between his teeth. Fearing, as my own mother was to fear years later, that her husband might destroy her child, Lupercalia, in one of those symbolically ritual acts, shot him, and after giving him a decent Christian burial, came with my father, then only an infant, to the new country.

How she managed to support him remains a mystery which my father belligerently refused to divulge although from a word dropped here and there, I am able to assume that it had something to do with my grandmother's more than casual understanding of the bestial needs of men. It is not from my father anyhow, but from my mother that I have learned the few remaining facts of the story. Lupercalia, feeling that she had given up so much for my father, was despotically possessive of him and, at the time of my father's announcement of his marriage intentions, she implored him not to leave her. Her grief took on, as the end of this story will bear out, classically tragic proportions.

On the day that my father broke the news of the engagement to her, Lupercalia fell to the floor, grabbed the cuff of his trousers and allowed herself to be dragged down the second floor hallway as he walked on firm of purpose. It was Providence that prevented her being hauled down the steps. Her dress caught on a nail in the molding just at the head of the staircase; and, seeing that her skirt had ripped, she allowed her discipline as the former wife of a missionary to surface. Ashamed at her indecent exposure in front of her son, she offered one last plea and then abandoned him in the name of modesty.

She chose, however, not to appear at the wedding, but returned instead to the little village of Tamburackoo, sacrificing herself to the offspring of the same lions that had enjoyed her first husband, this last act of self-abnegation revealed in a sealed letter left on my mother's bed by my grandmother and performed at the precise moment of the marriage of my parents themselves.

• • • • •

My maternal ancestry is a trifle less vague, though no less perverse. What details exist I learned from my Aunt Carole who alone dared reveal the secret when I went to visit her in the asylum on my seventh birthday. She and my mother were two of twenty-six children, each named for a different letter of the alphabet, conceived and produced by two very brave people who chose to play this little game of procreation to hide from each other the direst knowledge that each possessed. For my maternal grandparents it appears were a long lost twin brother and sister, each of whom apparently realized the secret on his and her wedding night because of a starfish birthmark that each had known the other had. However, each feared that the truth might drive the other mad; and so strong was the love they bore one another that each kept the realization locked in his and her heart, preferring slowly to lose his and her own sanity rather than to be the cause of the other's mental derangement. Accordingly, each, to deceive the other, elaborated intricate stories about a fictitious heritage, and each pretended to want a large number of children so that the other would not suspect his and her own terror at perpetuating this family heritage.

My Aunt Carole confesses to learning their secret too late to be able to secure from either of them any information which would lead to some exact understanding of their parentage. As she pointed out, what she did learn, she learned after the fact of their lives in a manner so horrendous as to drive further thoughts of pursuing their lineage from her mind.

On the cell wall of the asylum to which my grandmother was committed after the birth of the twenty-sixth child, under her barred window where the words could be deciphered only when the full quarter moon shone into the cell, Aunt Carole read the following confession which my grandmother had written in her own blood with a finger severed by her own hand in one lucid moment before hanging herself:

My husband, he a sister had
who, for love of husband,
let her brother's wife go mad.

And, in my grandfather's cell (the two had chosen
death as fate had given them life, on the same day and
in exactly the same manner), in a similarly hidden recess,
similarly written in identical blood, Aunt Carole found
the verse which told the rest of the story:

My wife, her brother's mark of birth she bore
which, as her husband, his sister's brother
did love more.

It may rightly be supposed that it was in the cell
just between the two occupied by her mother and father
that Aunt Carole came to her self-inflicted end, contribut-
ing her own verse to that vast body of the poetry of the
insane:

My parents, they a child bred
(brother–sister in their bed)
who honors now their secret shames
and further truck with life disdains.

• • • • •

Each of the twenty-six children of my maternal grandparents was to feel the weight of the family curse. Perhaps the most typical illustration was the grim drama which involved Cousin Patricia, daughter of the thirteenth child of the star-crossed siblings, Melancholia, who herself was born with a spray of rue in her hand.

When she was fourteen years old, Cousin Patricia found herself *in trouble*, a situation which threw the entire family into a preposterous uproar since it had been hoped that the misfortune which had plagued our ancestors would have worked itself out by the second generation. The uproar was confounded when it was revealed by Cousin Patricia that her male partner was none other than Freddie Washington, whom the family regarded as bad blood since his father had just been executed for the murder of his wife.

"The sins of the father are visited upon the son," moaned Melancholia, referring to the crime of Freddie's father.

"You just can't make a silk purse out of a sow's ear," nodded my mother in agreement.

Now nobody, except my father, had stopped to observe that Freddie Washington was only six and that, under the circumstances, his having impregnated Cousin Patricia was, to say the least, a physiological impossibility. The truth of the matter was that Cousin Patricia had used Freddie's name only to be as absurd in dealing with the family as they were in dealing with her situation.

"If only her father were here to defend her honor," wept Melancholia, "instead of having been blown to bits in the war. War is such a terrible terrible thing."

"It divides us all," agreed my mother tensely, reminding herself of the feud which had arisen between her sister and my father at the time that the body of Melancholia's husband had been sent home from the war. As it happened my father had been unable to attend the funeral, having the same day suffered a heart attack, and Melancholia never forgave him. He, feeling unjustly condemned, never forgave her for not forgiving him.

And now, to add insult to injury, my father disclosed quite casually that my mother's relatives were idiots, that Freddie Washington could not have sired Patricia's unborn child since he was only six years old. The family immediately became aware of the oversight, and, individually embarrassed, they collectively refused to admit their error, maintaining that they had merely pretended to believe Patricia's story in the hope that she, feeling that her true lover's name was safe, would carelessly reveal it. But, of course, Patricia had understood from the beginning that the family would not long accept the story that Freddie Washington had planted the seed in her, and she continued now to be as wary as ever.

Tension mounted until the baby was born and for seventeen years thereafter until the infant had emerged into a bloom of a girl, at which time she fell in love with Freddie Washington who was now twenty-three.

However, as might be expected, Freddie had never forgiven Cousin Patricia for using his name lightly, since the discussion of his quite normal lack of virility at six had made him so self-conscious of his sexual development that the process had actually been retarded — and only now did Freddie feel himself able to function with any degree of satisfaction. Determined to revenge himself upon Patricia and on our house, he seduced the girl once suspected of having been his daughter, my illegitimate second cousin, Ophelia.

Patricia, horrified at the manner in which the circle was being completed, beat her daughter senseless, causing a miscarriage which resulted in Ophelia's death. Then, overcome with grief at what she had done and as a kind of retribution against her mother's lineage, Patricia murdered her mother, Melancholia, damning her and her kind to wander endlessly among the shades for having brought her into the world. Finally, holding her mother's withered spray of rue next to her own heart, she took her life. Patricia used her dying breath to confess that it was ironically enough Freddie's father, whom she had visited in prison the night before his execution, who had been her lover and Ophelia's natural father.

As many of my readers know, I have spent some of my years as a playwright and already you must recognize that my comedy, *The House of Melancholia*, is based on this tale of incest, murder and suicide. I shall not now deal with the *why* of my having chosen to cast the story as a comedy. Those interested may go to my essay,

"Comic Inversions of Basically Tragic Themes," but for those who may be unfamiliar with the play, I shall briefly outline its variance with the true life story.

The first act follows the facts quite closely. However, as the play develops, it is revealed that Freddie's father was not guilty of murdering his wife; rather it was his wife's lover who did so, and that Freddie himself was genuinely in love with Ophelia and did not seduce her out of revenge. At the end of the second act, Cousin Patricia consents to a marriage between Ophelia and Freddie; and, in the third act, she enters into a love affair with the ghost of Freddie's father. The whole hilarious denouement joyously plays itself out on a midsummer's eve when the ghost of Freddie's father winks at Ophelia just after Patricia and Freddie have gone out into the garden.

CHAPTER THREE
L'enfant Perdu
mais pas Oublié

My mother was not one to leave my cultural development to chance as the decor of the nursery will testify. The ceiling of my room was papered with a reproduction of the Sistine Chapel while along the crib wall were placed illustrations from the original productions of *Medea, Oedipus Rex, Antigone, The School for Scandal* and Shakespeare's Chronicle Plays, most particularly, *Henry IV, Part I* — also a bust of Pan blowing his pipes in the direction of the east wall which was devoted to music and where I gazed upon Orpheus playing his lyre; Handel, in his nightshirt fingering his clavichord at the critical moment of his father's discovery of him; Bach and eleven of his children singing the first rough draft of the *B Minor Mass*; and Beethoven, in a moment of ecstasy, as deaf he hears the glorious finale of the *Ninth*. There were also on this wall cross-section drawings of the gourd, the xylophone, the tambourine, and the oboe d'amore. The north wall displayed the architecture of civilizations as revealed in the architecture of their buildings; and here the ruins of the Forum were placed in juxtaposition to the crumbling walls of Jericho, the Houses of Parliament with the Coliseum, while the city of Pompeii was pointedly laid at right angles to Westminister Abbey. On the west wall were two groupings whose whole did not equal the sum of their parts: the first included the feet of Pavlova, the scales of Justice, Madame and Pierre Curie engagés, Marco Polo, the Venus de Milo, Lillian Russell, Buddha and the Leaning Tower of Pisa; the second, an illuminated page of the *Ancrene Riwle*, four aspen leaves next to a butterfly under glass, a replica of the first wheel and a picture of George Washington crossing the Delaware.

But it was the floor of my room that haunted me. It was a representation of the nine circles of Dante's Inferno. My mother daily counseled: disregard the voices of the ceiling, the challenge of the walls, and you will find yourself consigned to the hell fires beneath this very floor.

● ● ● ● ●

If my mother was to bludgeon me nigh to death with the cultural values of life, my Aunt Carole, during those early years she was with me, chose to show me that in death there was also joy. Aunt Carole would tell me of the dead she had known. She would pause before a grave and literally bring the deceased back to life.

There was Samuel Kitchelpop, whom she had loved silently and distantly, hoping in the bloom of his lifetime that his wife would die and that she would herself be asked to marry him and raise his children. Now, when she passed his grave, she would bend over and kiss the headstone and plead with me that while I lived, I must love passionately and that I must never allow myself to be left with only a gravestone of desire.

Slowly and sadly we would wend our way among the markers with Aunt Carole extending greetings to other of her friends until we came to Kitchelpop's grave. Their meetings were born of basic needs, and directly and forthrightly they spoke with one another. Only eleven elemental words were used: wind, air, light, water, earth, love, sky, sun, moon, stars, hate — to which occasionally were added terror and wonder as well as appropriate and sundry prepositions and articles. Wind connoted sadness, ferocity, passion, longing — according to its context; air: delicacy, coolness, joy — also warmth, hope, and understanding; water: smoothness, glitter, somberness, depth, constancy or fickleness when rippling was or was not intimated; earth: belonging, birth, death, possession; love: all manner of; fire: fury, desire, man's responsibility to man; sky: height, the extension of all life and death; sun, moon, and stars described the fixed unchangeables as well as master, mistress, and youth respectively; hate: all manner of; terror and wonder — as experienced.

"Air of the sun, fire!" Aunt Carole would whisper in greeting Kitchelpop on each occasion. (Loosely translated, she was lovingly announcing herself as the "Joy of her master's desire!")

"Earth, wind, love!" would come Kitchelpop's

answer from the grave. (Death is the sadness of love.)

"Stars! Stars! Stars!" I would cry impassioned, my ardent and insistent plea for youth.

"Sky!" Aunt Carole and Samuel Kitchelpop would wail together instead of so cumbersome an expression of their feeling as, "The extension of all life is death!"

"Water of hate is hate!" Aunt Carole would repeat over and over again, for she incessantly tried to absolve herself of the guilt of having wished Samuel's wife dead. (Notice the sudden and daring use of the verb — so startling because of the violence which tears at it, before and after.)

"Fire, earth, stars, wind-wind!" Samuel spoke understandingly. I have always marveled at Samuel's extraordinary power to give language beauty. The phrase literally means nothing.

But Samuel was using the first wind idiomatically, and his immediate repetition of it allowed the words the freest blown interpretation. How gently he was telling her, "Desire, my dearest, is born of youth — woebetide its passion!"

To which, with a heart-rending cry, Aunt Carole would whisper, "Oh, Samuel!"

• • • • •

I discovered my sex at an early age when, naked and losing my footing one afternoon, I grabbed for something to balance myself. There was instant pleasure.

I grabbed again and again and again, and in those three movements, I knew that I had discovered the sexual miracle of myself. How time and time over I was to elaborate on these gestures, fantasize with them, till, on occasion I was able to derive as much joy from an admiration at my creative manipulation as I was from the physiological and emotional release. On one occasion I so applauded my own performance that I drew a demand from my mother who was downstairs busily making dinner.

"Gregory," she shouted up to me, "whatever are you doing?"

Immediately I was assailed with guilt! Immediately I was afraid! I saw myself as a scoundrel and wastrel — about to denigrate my accomplishment with a blatant lie.

"I am — I am — applauding the genius of Socrates," I called, holding my privates shamefully in my hands.

"Good child, good child," she said, "but Socrates, being dead, cannot enjoy your plaudits, so use your energies to read on."

Immediately I looked down at my limpness and, associating the death of Socrates with the collapse of my member, a new and somewhat morbid intensity associated itself with my sexual flights: was I, in truth, by tampering with this source of life not also tampering with the powers of death — was death not implicit in life — was there never to be undiluted pleasure for me — was the entire ambivalence of my existence to be epitomized in this simple act of self-expression. God! God! wonder of misery, I thought, as I flung my naked shivering body into the hell fires of the second circle there on the floor of my room. Indeed, the hell fires themselves seemed to consume my flesh as they have continued to do with my profoundest enjoyments of the triumphs of lust.

So are the strands of memory and the tribulations of life woven together. So are love and death, love in death, death in life, and life in love inextricably intertwined. Would all woe be severed from joy that pleasure might be unto itself a thing of things — but rats and roses, being what they are, there is no end to collusion.

CHAPTER FOUR
Pandora's Box

When I was two, I was given pottery lessons to develop small muscle control. When I was three, piano lessons were added; at four, violin; at five, dancing lessons; at six, fencing and skating; at seven, polo and Yoga; at eight, the flute, trumpet and French horn; at nine, pottery was dropped, and oils included while dancing was increased by a session and Hindustani introduced; at ten, skating and the French horn were eliminated, only to be replaced by two drama classes and mandolin appreciation. Mother was eager to achieve some tactical balance of stresses, strains, and insights; and at September time each year, she consulted Dr. Kinderplast, my child psychologist, for a new program for the new season.

Dr. Kinderplast was a grasshopper of a man, who was constantly thrusting his arms up and down and in and out, expanding, as he said, his personal domain. One must not live enclosed, he would constantly mutter, mumble, or shriek, according to the weather — but one should always fight the circumference of his territorial imperative. I rather enjoyed my sessions with Dr. Kinderplast whom I called Fanny for short.

My first meeting with Fanny came about as a result of my having, at the age of three, strangled my sister. Mother, quite naturally, kept the murder a secret, shoving my sister's head through the bars of her crib and appalling the police with an hysterical account of a violent accident. She explained to the police that, as if perceiving the tragedy a month before it happened, she had already conceived another child. And then, after serving them quiche noire, venison à la Rambeau, artichoke favors and torte renversé along with Pueblo ritual wine, she got them to leave, closing the door and the case appreciatively behind them.

But posthaste she rushed me to Dr. Kinderplast, who alone knew our secret, and who, during our first session, revealed to me the bloody path he had trod to adulthood. It was his contention, he announced, his arms flaying up and down and in and out, that one must survive at all costs. He reassured me that he would help me deal with my sister's death, turn it into a positive force in my life, a quintessential experience from which I might derive an appreciation of flesh, blood and Fourierism. Wickedly he laughed and, grabbing me closely to him, he rocked and wept and howled himself to sobbing silence. I kissed him gently and tiptoed from the room.

Needless to say, as time went on Fanny became more and more dependent on me; soon he was increasing the number of visits so that he could derive as much benefit as possible from my services. In time I insisted that he turn over to me the fees my mother was paying him, and soon I requested that he raise his fees. Eventually, my desire for money grew upon itself and inspired me to greed; I decided that what my mother was paying him was simply not enough for me to survive on so I got myself a job with Mr. Horace who owned a grocery store just seven blocks from our home.

• • • • •

Since my extra-curricular studies allowed me no time for after-school work, I was obliged once again to turn the exigencies of my life to my own purposes and resort to duplicity. Appreciating the fact that every man has his price, I bribed each of my after-school teachers by promising a goodly addition to his weekly grocery order and, so that my mother would not suspect my absenteeism, assiduous practice in his particular area of instruction if each of them would grant me release time to take the position. To receive their regular lesson payment, supplementary groceries and to have my allotted hour to take on another pupil (although Mr. Winsome who taught me mandolin appreciation had, as might be expected, no other pupils) was enticement enough for them. They all agreed, and I went happily to my first employment.

However, I could not risk identification by any of our neighbors nor even fleeting notice by a member of my family. I had somehow to devise a means whereby I could move freely without recognition. My flair for the dramatic came to my rescue. Wearing a half mask, a remnant from a discarded Halloween costume, I was able to carry out my duties undetected, and, ipso facto, soon I became known as the masked delivery boy. Capitalizing on the excitement attendant to the success of my disguise, I purchased several dissimilar masks and alternated them to the delight of my public. The degree of anticipation which marked my appearance was soon rewarded with proportionately larger tips and the ardent request that I make each house the first on the following day's delivery schedule.

I am ashamed to say I took advantage of the generous nature of some of my customers. I remember one old lady who asked me why I wore the mask, and realizing she believed it concealed some tragic aspect of my life, I told her I had been burned as an infant, that my face was atrociously disfigured and that I could not bear to have people look directly upon me. This more than satisfied her suspicions and complimented her belief in her acute powers of perception and inference. From then on, her compassion knew no remunerative restraint, and frequently the token which she accorded me was even in excess of the amount of her purchase. With still greater qualms of conscience, I confess to further exploitation of her generosity, sometimes dividing her order into three loads, for she would not have me leave the door, even three times within the hour, without some reminder of her sympathy. My talent for the theatric was paying off splendidly in this first encounter with a live audience, and soon I was drawing more from Mr. Horace's business than he himself.

However, even at this early age the wearing of these masks and the deception incumbent upon the act were playing havoc with my soul. It would take several hours at the end of each working day for me to discover my self which had been so artfully concealed. What endless torment this was to cause me then, and even now when I seek the discovery of my self for years hidden under life's successive masks! I recall Aunt Carole's telling me, "Remember, Gregory, Sun of the Wind is as the air of the sun, moon and sun sun!" How basic is this precept: "The master of all true passion is the joy of the uncorrupted self — changeless, honest to itself, no matter what the follies with which its physical being is plagued!"

It was not long before I was earning so much more from Mr. Horace's business than he was that he was forced to sell out to me, a situation which caused his attempted suicide. But still I was not satisfied. With the callowness of youth and the bravado of my triumph, I demanded that he use his life-savings to convert his grocery store into a little theatre and that he indenture himself to me. I named the theatre for Aunt Carole — calling it quite unabashedly the AUNT CAROLE — and while it looked somewhat incongruous standing between Darlington's Fish Market and Polakoff's Hardware, it could not have looked more glorious to me had it been in the very heart of the theatre district.

CHAPTER FIVE
Laissez-faire but Art

Before I go on, I must go back!

The murder of my first sister made me extremely leery of the birth of a new child. My mother explained that she would not be able to lie away a second murder, and I must condition myself to the fact that there would be a brother or sister in the house. We decided to prepare me for the event with a series of spiritual exercises.

My mother bought a doll and placed it in what was to be the baby's room. She had me look in on the doll several times a day, talk to it, and even buy it presents. Egregiously the inevitable happened; I fell in love with the doll and the thought of anyone's taking her place drove me to fury. (Demon! oh demon that you are, did you really contemplate bringing about your mother's miscarriage!) I tried desperately to conceal my passion, but one day as I held Lucia to me, my father passed the room. Sickened by what he felt was my lack of manliness to begin with and seeing me now with a doll held compromisingly in my arms, he grabbed Lucia and flung her to the floor. I swooned. My mother, beside herself with anger, anguished for my shock and the gloomy premonition that forthcoming events cast their shadows before them, seemed to lose her mind. She tackled my father, and having him beneath her, proceeded to pummel him till I thought he was lifeless. I hesitated between being perfectly willing to see her succeed in his murder and knowing somewhere in the recesses of my being that he could yet serve my purposes if only as a foil in dealing with my mother's excesses. With a daring lunge, I tore my mother from him and then, hoisting him over my shoulders, I carried him from the room, placing him in a heap in the bathtub and turning on the warm water to bathe his wounds. The moment he seemed to revive, I hurried back to my mother who, on her hands and knees, had now collected all the smitherins that had been Lucia.

"We'll show him!" she vowed, and pushing me ahead of her, she hurried me into the kitchen. Painstakingly we glued Lucia together, and while I dreaded the emerging image of the cracked face and body, I soon sensed the profoundest empathy for the mutilated self, and my love for Lucia gorgeously burgeoned as I slipped the tiniest fragments of her lips into place. As a result, it is their scars and deformities that have attracted me to the women I have loved, and I unrighteously confess that I have lost track of the number of rare beauties who, becoming aware of my penchant, have deliberately disfigured themselves to gain my embrace.

Lucia once again in my possession, I nervously awaited the birth of my sister, even precipitating her birth by throwing my mother into premature labor after I inadvertently (yes! it was inadvertently) mixed up some bottles in the medicine chest. Arriving early, my sister ever after blamed her somewhat delayed responses and slow learning abilities on the fact that my error with the medicine bottles had deprived her of a full uterine development, while I logically tried to explain to her that, given more time to develop in that ancestrally doomed environment which had probably caused her dysfunctions, her brain damage might have been even more severe.

Unable to think of any name we were eager to call the babe, my mother settled on Wilma, the name of the nurse who attended her in the hospital — a narrow lady who offered her own name to all the bewildered mothers who couldn't think of one for their daughters and her husband's name of Granger to all who found themselves without names for their sons. For the accommodation of using the name, my mother granted Wilma and Granger visiting rights, but they unfortunately abused the privilege, Wilma's kleptomaniacal tendencies compelling her to attempt kidnapping my sister, and Granger on one occasion trying to rape my mother so he might reestablish a balance of power by having her conceive a male child who might rightfully bear his own name.

My sister's witlessness appealed to my father from the instant he laid eyes on her. Here truly was his life's companion, and he was determined to hold her as closely to him as my mother was grasping at me. Asserting his prerogatives, he would not allow my mother to care for her but instead carried her back and forth to work with him in a meticulously appointed bird cage, placing her beside him on the bench in the gum-labeling factory where he tediously licked ornate labels onto oddly shaped and sized bottles. My mother, suffering the loss of her daughter's presence so immediately upon giving birth to her, turned once more to Lucia whom she persuaded me to take from my hiding place under my shirt. Again the inevitable happened; my mother and I decided to ignore my father and Wilma completely, and we set up under the same roof a household of our own, I soon losing my relationship as a son and becoming my mother's mate in all but name. However, since we were each vergingly aware of the horrendous implications of our relationships, at our closest there was distance between us, and we were as four strangers.

Now it will become obvious why I have filled in this background. The first play performed at the AUNT CAROLE was originally called *Four Strangers* (immediately changed to *Guise of Strangers*) though years later it was revised under the more exact title, *You, the Thought of Me, The Father and the Girl*. In its original form, it is a stinging denunciation of family life; in my more mature years I was able to heighten its Greek overtones, enhancing the tragic waste of all life by having it performed in the city dump.

• • • • •

Certainly between the establishment of the AUNT CAROLE and the opening of *Guise of Strangers*, né *Four Strangers*, my existence was not a simple one. The immediate reaction of my family to my enterprise was enervating. My mother never quite recovered from the realization that for two years I had deceived her by cutting out of my afternoon lessons; my father was scandalized that my theatric tendencies, which he regarded as unmanly, were progressing; and my sister, who was unable to remember her own name under the best of circumstances, walked about the house believing that all this talk of Carole applied to her. Eventually, unable to simplify matters by the expedient desecration of calling Wilma by Carole's name, my father ran away, leaving Wilma in a catatonic state and my mother decimated with guilt and confusion, threatening self-slaughter.

Now you must realize how impossible any creative efforts would be under such circumstances; so refusing to allow anything to interfere at this time with the accomplishment of my goals, I decided to restore order as quickly as possible by seeking out my father — what trembling significance there is to these words! — and bringing him home.

Within three days after I had begun my search, I found him at Hammond's Gymnasium. Not really having the courage to run away, he had spent the three days on a stationary bicycle pedaling himself to exhaustion. I told him that while I bore him no love, his daughter was lost without him and his wife nearly mad with grief. He struck me down and then stood evilly over me. I cannot say what possessed me, but for one brief moment, I wanted his love. I wanted him to pick me up and shower upon me some of the affection of which he had so consistently deprived me. Knowing that unless he was deceived, he would never hold me even for a moment, I resorted to my talents as an actor: I held my breath and let my mouth fall open so that I might convey the idea that he had rendered me near to lifeless. Perhaps it was fear that he had harmed me and would suffer at the hand of the law rather than any fleeting desire, but he did kneel beside me and take my hand. He was feeling for my pulse, and I knew that as soon as he had located it, he would be satisfied and let go. I could not bear this. So I moaned low and painfully, "Where is my father. I want my father!" I was not to realize the enormous impact of these words till years later when on one splintering afternoon in the office of Dr. Fuerhrerstein, I started to climb up the clothes rack, and Dr. Fuerhrerstein, with a malevolent understanding, smiled and said, "You must come down, Gregory! You must come down! The clothes rack is not your father's knee nor anything else that is your father's!" But all I knew on that hot afternoon in Hammond's Gymnasium was that my plea had its effect. I felt my father's hand tremble, and like some lover fumblingly touching the body of his mistress for the first time, he moved his hand to my face. I did not dare open my eyes to see the devotion I believed was suffusing his features, for I knew that I had tricked him into a demonstration of emotion and that if he became aware of my deception, I would lose the moment. The truth of the matter is that I have never been able to see such a light in my father's eyes because, wanting to savor that moment I did not venture to realize it. What a heartless paradox — only by depriving myself of this vision could I possibly secure it.

In a moment he picked me up and cradled me close to him. I smelled the sweat on his naked body and my cheek touched his bare wet chest. I must have winced because he dropped me. The incompleteness of that embrace, the severing of even this invalid bond between us was to have a profound influence on me. As I later realized, I have endured much humiliation trying to complete that demonstration of affection — all with tragic consequences. (Oh! Immanuel, my love! You above all the others know the significance of these words! How often I made you sweat! But you alone carried the scent! Compulsively, I turned you into an animal! — — — Dear God! Suddenly! Now I understand what I have never understood before! Lupercalia! — the pride of lions — the turning of Immanuel, my lover, into an animal, carrying that smell of my father's ancestry back into that lion's den near that little village of Tamburackoo! When you disappeared, Immanuel — I never thought to look where no men go!)

• • • • •

Success in the theatre is helped by chance. And, in the next ten minutes, there in Hammond's Gymnasium, I was to have my first brush with this whimsy, for into the locker room came Appleton Howard White. I knew that at the moment he was appearing in no play, and I fancied that if I could persuade him to act at the AUNT CAROLE, my initial venture would be assured of glory.

On first sight, the legendary strength of his personality was obvious to me. There was a hypnotic ugliness to his face. Instantly I remembered the stories of his indifference to adulation, of his demoniac attack at the core of a role, of his compulsive grit in uncovering every shade and shiver of a character. I watched as he changed into his workout clothes and was suddenly acutely conscious of the fact that he was watching me watch him. I knew I must speak.

"Mr. Appleton Howard White," I began, having no idea how to go on.

He did not answer, but only stared at me, his eyes onyx and lonely.

"I have a little theatre," I said, quaking at my presumptuousness. "It is called the AUNT CAROLE. It is yet to produce its first play. Would you perform in it?"

What naiveté! What boldness! I could not bring myself to think what I would say if he asked me about the play I had in mind.

"I never mix business with gymnastics," he said cryptically, "but if you will visit me at ten o'clock tomorrow morning, we can talk." And with that, he handed me his card, brushed by me and out through the locker room doors to the gym.

I could not grasp the fact that he had not said NO! But what would I propose to him the next morning! What play could I offer him!

• • • • •

I had less than eight hours to complete the play I would show to Appleton Howard White — or at least enough of it to convince him of the necessity of appearing at the AUNT CAROLE. I have always done my best work under pressure, and it was with boundless joy that I now attacked my task. Certain factors immediately made themselves clear. Although the play would concern my family, I would have to shuffle our roles in order to get far enough away from my material to be able to turn it into theatre. Writing about my father as he was or my mother as she was involved me much too deeply in the personal reality of the situation and would further provide me with little of the adventure of discovery so imperative to creating any substantial work of art. So I decided quite simply to turn everything inside out: I would make my father my mother, my mother my father; my sister and I with mammoth changes of motivation would switch roles — and my Aunt Carole would become Samuel Kitchelpop.

Right off I had solved one of the most pressing of my problems: an off-line but sympathetic role (with sinister subtext) for Appleton Howard White — he would play my father transposed mother. My mother, of course, was now a totally unpleasant character, imbued as she was with all of my father's worst attributes. My sister, a struggling artist, who, in real life, would have hated my father, now, of course, loved him because he was more her mother than her father as I, now my spiritual sister, hated my mother, who, in the world of drama, was really my father. By a stroke of genius I was able to maintain superb objectivity while keeping the physical relationships the same; however, the audiences who believed they were seeing a familiar father-son, mother-daughter struggle were in for a big surprise since my sister only loved her father because she was her brother and he (her father) was really her mother, and I only loved my mother because in truth she was my father and I was my sister! On the other hand, unable even fictitiously to live without respite in the form of my sister, I added to my character the role of the Greek chorus.

I decided further to compress the action of the play so that it covered a period of eight hours, cutting down the Aristotelian allowance for time unity by thirds. And since the activity of our waking moments often belies our primal feelings and motives, I further decided to set the play at night while the characters slept. Accordingly, in a Prologue of ten sections, each of the characters said "Goodnight" to one another: the father to the mother, the father to the daughter, the father to the son, and the father to the uncle (an added character whose ambiguities were intended to do homage to both Aunt Carole and Appleton Howard White); the mother to the son, the mother to the daughter, the mother to the uncle; the sister to the brother, the sister to the uncle and the uncle to his nephew. Kitchelpop, knowing that he was really Aunt Carole, bridged the Prologue and the first act by embracing himself in a self-abnegating mime which also signaled the curtain to rise!

Each of these brief scenes — bristling with the tensions of their individual subtexts but using the same lines of dialogue, "Goodnight, I'll see you in the morning," showed starkly the meaninglessness of all words and set the sweltering mood of this untoward tragedy.

When I finished the Prologue, I was shaken. My face burned — my lips were dry — my heart pounded — the entire play breathed. I had succeeded with a minimum of dialogue in setting a mood so tense I could barely hold pencil to Act One.

As the curtain rose, six people were discovered sleeping — but the very conception of the scene was symbolic. No ordinary sleep was this — instead the characters were nimbly seated on mechanical elephants moving on belts — (elephants for me meant India, India for me meant the survival of ancient mysteries and the upsurgings of primitive memory and love) — at oblique angles to one another and haphazardly as if they were manifestations of themselves in one another's minds. The stage directions were explicit in underscoring the rhythms of their movements — nothing in unison — emphatically diagramming the lack of unity in their lives — even their breathing must be syncopated, and the spastic jerking, tossing and turning of an irregularity that defied pattern or resolution. The jagged effect of the charging elephants was further enhanced by there being no single source of stage lighting — but at each seat in the theatre in a special case (into which each member of the audience placed a quarter) there was a flashlight. By playing his own flashlight where he chose, each member of the audience could participate as he wished, living through the nightmares of the characters with whom he most strongly empathized. The physical participation of each member of the audience made for the release of his own haunting subconscious urgings and created a general uproar, an extension of the play's basic theme and a visualization in graphic terms of squelched souls in Hell. My play was all things to all men and one thing to each man. And, further, I was able to charge twenty-five cents on top of the price of admission.

• • • • •

But as every playwright knows, a drama cannot survive merely on devices for stimulating mood nor, for that matter, on ingenious stage trickery. There must be some conflict — something which drives the play forward and draws the audience to involvement. The basic plot of *Four Strangers* concerned the efforts of each member of the family to remain asleep without ever waking to a torment worse than that which he was undergoing. They were not courting the sleep that is death — but rather the sleep of life — a sleep which would allow them to live without being conscious of one another.

However, in order to live one must be able to act (what an ironic interplay — and yet still another trenchant pun): to eat, to drink, to work, to take care of personal functions — and to manage these things in a perpetual state of somnolence would, of course, demand the most supreme struggle. The conflict of my play so clearly established, the broad meanings of its story became bold and basic. Was this not the fundamental battle of everyman's attempt to stay alive and still escape the realities of his life which destroyed his peace of mind. By vividly underscoring the desire for withdrawal without resorting to such tried and true means as alcohol, narcotics, or sex, I knew I was dealing with a subject of enormous import while at the same time keeping it from ever becoming trite or sordid; for, in this dream world, each of the characters, coming more closely in touch with his id than he could in a waking life, soon learned that he was not in truth who he thought he was, as of course, who of us is!

The device of sleep now served as a vital dramatic force: should they all awaken and realize the deceptions they had played upon one another, how could they possibly face the morning life. The struggle to remain asleep became vital to their very existence. But the Fates were not to be so kind: the cock soon crowed — the sun soon broke through the clouds, the elephants on the moving belts halted, the flashlights went out, the houselights went up as the characters on the stage, horrified, stared nakedly at one another while, in the audience, wife broke from the embrace of brother, father guiltily pushed son from him and daughter heaved uncle from her arms. The silence of shame gripped the opening night audience.

"End it! End the torment and the torture! Bring down the curtain on the damnably unsettling play! shouted one member of the audience. Racing to the footlights, he pleaded to be released — and, one after another, like supplicants at a confession, the audience fell upon its knees. (The theatre had indeed returned to its religious origins.) The characters on stage, joining hands and moving with the slow sure tread of the Fates which had encouraged the dawn, met the audience head on, bowing deeply and with bitter though compassionate laughter, said only "Goodmorning!"

If you will recall, I mentioned that years later I darkened the play, presenting it under the title *You, The Thought of Me, the Father and the Girl*. The device I used must now be apparent to you: I played the action during the waking moments with all the characters trying to fall asleep — and their trials and tribulations were diabolically exposed by the inordinately complex but telling shenanigans they used to bring themselves to slumber. No mere counting of sheep could these folk use! The triumph of this play is, as you all know, legendary!

• • • • •

The play finished, I washed, dressed and walked to the house noted on the card Appleton Howard White had given me. (From now on I will refer him as Haw-Haw, a name used by only his closest associates and artfully formed by a convenient transposition of his initials.) I was shocked when I arrived at a twelve-story tenement where Haw-Haw had persuaded the landlord to let him construct a roof dwelling so he could show his disdain for superstitions which forbid thirteenth-floor habitation. He further demonstrated his disregard for the worldly show to which his outstanding success entitled him by constructing and furnishing his apartment with pieces of junk purchased from junkyards around the world. It was as if the visitor was approaching a superb collage — no monotonous line to the dwelling inside or out — each object doing double duty by its placement, the pieces being set facing inside or out according to the practical advantages to be gained: so a marble coffee table laid with the marble facing out was a startling fortress of an exterior while the legs of the table protruded boldly into the house serving as a coat rack.

Now perhaps the most amazing part of the story! When I arrived at Haw-Haw's apartment, he looked tense — wild-eyed — almost terrified — like one who has undergone some violent ordeal which has unnerved him. He opened the automobile door which served as the door and sat staring at me from the driver's seat. Then, with the same quality of unearthly mocking compassionate laughter called for in the final directions of *Four Strangers,* he said, "Goodmorning."

Our eyes met, and I could scarcely hold the manuscript in my hand. I had the feeling that Haw-Haw knew what *Four Strangers* was about — and even more that he had suffered through its composition with me. And I was right — by this extraordinary sympatico which was to bind us inseparably for years, this miracle had come to pass. I needed to relate none of the plot to him, I needed to read none of the dialogue to him. He knew it all. He had — separated from me by the city of lost souls — found mine. And now, no sooner did I pass over the doorstep — three exquisitely carved ram horns set into a section of corrugated box — than Haw-Haw took me into his arms — like my father for whom I had been searching for years — and said with ardent passion: "It is a beautiful, beautiful play — and you are a beautiful, beautiful rose of a boy, and I love your play, and I love your smell — and the father and the son and the son and the father will continue to search for one another unto and throughout eternity, and only in the guise of strangers will they meet."

Accordingly, the new title, *Guise of Strangers*!

• • • • •

Haw-Haw was a man obsessed. Orphaned at the age of three, he had suffered a childhood of deprivation. Fleeing from the authorities rather than endure surrogate parents, he had hidden himself in the woods, surviving on plant life, insects, and birds which had been attacked and neglected by their predators. It was in these woods that he met Melissa, also a child of nature, whose parents had abandoned her in the care of a pygmy nursemaid with whom Haw-Haw immediately fell in love. Amelia, as the nursemaid was called, anticipating that Haw-Haw would lose his affection for her as he grew to manhood and learned that what charmed him now would only be considered a deformity as he himself developed in size, attempted to amputate his legs. Melissa, in an act of instinctive heroism, threw herself at Amelia, losing her left ear as Amelia recklessly slashed with the knife. Both children, understanding that Amelia was not now to be trusted, conspired to murder her, which they did, burying her unceremoniously in the decayed remains of a fallen tree.

But Amelia was not to be dealt with so summarily. Within hours after Amelia's death, Haw-Haw noticed a change in Melissa. She began to shrink till she was no taller than Amelia had been, and soon her movements became loose and spastic; within a day she threw herself on the ground and howled to be spared further punishment.

"It's that witchgirl, Amelia," Melissa gurgled. "She's got hold of me."

Haw-Haw tried to help Melissa. He tried feeding her red herbs which he found under bushes; he tried making her potions with feathers, dewdrops, pods and bees; he tried uttering all sorts of incantations, but nothing availed. Finally in a remote moment of despair, he took her in his arms. She seemed suddenly to grow savagely desirous of him; excited by her orgiastic screams he made love to her; then she quieted and from her passion-dried lips he heard the mocking voice of Amelia, satisfied and whispering rapturously that she would possess him through Melissa forever and ever.

Unable to bear Melissa's intense suffering, unwilling to be dominated by Amelia's vengeful nature, Haw-Haw had no choice but to destroy Melissa for whom he had developed the most inflamed devotion. Hoping to forbid Amelia's escape through Melissa's last breath, Haw-Haw suffocated his beloved with a death-dealing kiss, watching peace suffuse her face as Amelia's anima expired. Then, as he laid Melissa to rest, he vowed that, having deprived her of mortal life, he would assure her of immortality, dedicating himself to her glory like some medieval knight whose lady's wish was his harkening.

"Your play, my boy, will give me the chance to dwell with Melissa again," he wept with blissful tears.

Carried along with his fervor, I cried, "Two of us shall realize our immortality. And shall use that glory to decorate our ladies! Benedicta Melissa! Salve Aunt Carole!"

No sooner had I spoken than Haw-Haw and I heard

a mingled laughter, a crystalline duet of two joyous feminine voices, and we knew that as we held each other, ecstatic in the perfection of our early beings, so Melissa and Aunt Carole had joined in divine embrace beyond ourselves in the perfect empyrean realms to which we aspired.

• • • • •

Such was the heavenly blessing of our joint venture. And this propitious beginning was not to be marred. Melissa and Aunt Carole worked with us, daily firing our imaginations. *Guise of Strangers* opened to critical and popular praise, the press unanimously bestowing encomiums on Haw-Haw, not only for his performance but for his daring for undertaking a role in a play by an unknown grocery boy. The lead sentence of the front page *Times* article read: "Appleton Howard White is to be hailed not only for his dazzling interpretation of an extraordinary role in *Guise of Strangers,* but also for his intuitive gifts which urged him to participate in such a history-making theatrical event."

Though I had dreamed of such acclaim, I was, alas! unprepared for it. And I plunged into devouring despair. The end of the struggle, the abrupt release of tension, the delirium of adulation, the assault on my privacy, and, as if this was not enough, the untoward behavior of my family! My mother, overreacting to the world's acknowledgment of my genius, became obstreperously manic, overturning the contents of the house while she screamed, "I knew it, I knew it, for the Lord Did Say Unto Me, 'Woman, out of thy Womb shall come not only The Poet but The Pen' "; my father's response was intensified: feeling that I had embarrassed all manhood and specifically destroyed whatever semblance of sense of worth he may have had, he enveloped himself in sackcloth and went into mourning; my sister, believing my father was mourning her, sought to gratify his wishes: she lay down in the middle of the living room floor as if dead, taking no food nor water, forcing us finally to hospitalize her.

Nor was I prepared to deal with Haw-Haw's bedevilment, which accompanied his triumph. "I have never, never known failure," he shouted, "Never in my life have I failed! It is the only experience of which I have been deprived, and I cannot endure this niggling limitation on my soul. I must fail, Gregory! Help me, help me, dear God, dear Gregory to fail." I tried to tell him that if he failed to fail, he would have failed in the grandest manner, but he pointed out that this failure he would never actually enjoy since his failure to fail could only come after the fact of his having lived.

The attack upon my senses could not be resisted, and I gave way. For once I allowed myself to become helpless; for once I luxuriated in my incapacity. And weeping hysterically, I beat at the doors of the Alabaster Home For The Insane and had myself committed.

PART TWO

Pilgrim's Progress

CHAPTER SIX

All those little men and all those little women— But where are the moths?

Everything in the Alabaster Home for the Insane was full of holes. The interior was constructed as a series of holes, designed to enhance our freedom. We walked through walls, dropped through floors, raised ourselves through ceilings and minimized our personal precipices by concentrating our sense of danger on balancing ourselves around the curved joinings. All feelings of guilt were removed as we spied easily on one another without the demeaning attitude of kneeling and peeping through keyholes. There was further the constant experience of rebirth as we moved through opening after opening, the inmates frequently screaming as if suffering the birth trauma while they jumped, plunged, tore or wriggled through the variously sized holes.

I myself spent hours lying curved in one circle or another, shaping myself to see the world in a succession of oblique perspectives, comfortably absorbed in meditations on the roundness of things. Soon I carried my preoccupation into movements, advancing now by walking in a series of interlocking circles, small to large,

large to small, hide and seek, hide and seek. Then I
elaborated the idea, revolving myself surreptitiously in
the slowest semblance of the darkest pirouette as I
completed each larger circle. Ultimately, I saw myself as
the earth, as the moon, even the stars moving about the
Sun. But soon this was disturbing me because I wanted
then to be the Sun and to have the planets of men revolve
about me. It was no time at all before I did indeed try to
be the Sun, three times setting myself afire, but having
no success in being able to ascend into my rightful place
in the Heavenly Spheres, I threw myself into the circles
of Hell which had dominated my life as a child.

Here in this fiery furnace I met Lavinia, who weeping
scalding tears, dared tell me her story. (*S'io credesse che
mia reposte fosse / A persona che mai tornasse al etceterata
indubliatata — !*) She came, she said, from a branch of
the Medicis, her family having been deprived of its
rightful heritage by the more notorious members of the
clan. She had been raped by her brother, Alfonzo Rienzi,
when she was seven, but instead of hating him for the
violation, she had fallen irresistibly and inconsolably in
love with him. When he had refused to take her as a
mistress, preferring her sister Incestiata, Lavinia joined
a nunnery, intending to mete out the rest of her life in
holy seclusion. But such was not to be her destiny. An
angel of God visited her and told her the Saints had
chosen her to go to Hell to suffer for the sins of Mankind.
And now, smiling beneficently as she spoke, Lavinia led
me solicitously through the labyrinth of the Underworld.

Everything that Dante had said was true. From every niche and cranny, crevice and corner, frightened burning souls popped their heads out at me.

"Beware!" they cried. "Beware! Leave while you can — contrary to belief, there are doors, you know!"

When I asked Lavinia about the doors, she merely shrugged. In all the years she had been burning here, she had never come upon any door, but the front door. Though she had heard other doors existed, she was certain they had existed only in the past. The hope of the haunted around me was, according to Lavinia, based on a legend that once some million years ago, one man had escaped through a hidden door, but then the Legions of Hell had removed this hidden door, leaving only those open circles through which we maddeningly passed back on ourselves. (*Ma perioche giammai questo fondo / non torno vivo alcunai, si'i'odo il vero, incrediable sans doubta —.*) She, of course, had never tried to search for the doors. As a Saint designate, she must remain in Hell until her Benefactors had Mercy on her or until Mankind sinned no more. Ave Maria! Amen!

With that said, Lavinia fainted in my arms, innocence in her eyes and savagery on her lips. I kissed those lips and the cries of the lost souls were hushed. I looked around and about and saw the fires quelled, the tears of the inmates having rained down upon them. Steam hissed, angelic choirs hosannahed, and the mocking Voice of the Devil echoed through the charred caverns. Agony and ecstasy in successive waves surged through me.

From that moment on, Lavinia and I possessed each other, her divided nature (Saint and Sinner) complementing my own rat-rose dichotomy. When my aggressive rat self was in ascendance, Lavinia gave her damned self to me; when I was my rosy best, I knew the seraph's touch. Only rarely were our two natures taken unawares. And there was perhaps no sight more awful than Gregory the Rat attacking the sanctified Lavinia or the gentle Rose being crushed by the tempestuous Mistress of Satan himself. For, most awful, part of Lavinia's curse was to have to capitulate to the lascivious demands of the Master of the Underworld.

I would know when Lavinia had been with him because at such times the Angels and Devils would engage in such caterwauling as would cause speculative confusion as to which was which, and the stars would burn in the fires of Hell and the flames, inspired, would reach up to embrace the moon. At such times I would try to hide myself from Lavinia, but wildly she would seek me out and inevitably I would be carried by her through the exploding effulgence to the most sulphurous corners of the deepest recesses of the darkest regions, where she would unleash on me the still active volcanic passions ranging from her encounter with the Malodorous Him. At such times I knew the very limits of madness, the stench and the dissonances of ruptured nightmares. (Angelina! Angelina! Pauvre petite!)

Inevitably Haw-Haw, who came to visit me daily, would intrude upon my intimacies with Lavinia.

"You are indiscreet, Haw-Haw," I would fume.

And Lavinia would fall prostrate before him, and thinking him one of the Saints who had placed his faith in her, she would beg him not to reveal her behavior to God. Haw-Haw would promise to keep her confidence and then, still not raising her head, she would drop through a hole to the floor below. Haw-Haw and I would look down on her and she up at us, and we would all three offer Silent Prayers.

When I was not with Lavinia or Haw-Haw, and when I was not meditating on the roundness of things, I played my flute, frequently finding myself followed by lines of the Insane who swayed and danced and leaped and sang to my music. On we would go through the openings from corridor to corridor, the excitement growing to frenzy, the frenzy to sensuality, the sensuality to Bacchanalian extravagances.

It was during one of these exhausting interludes that I had a vision of the Mountain Top of Gilmartisa where I saw the vague outlines of a man wrapped in a sheep's wool, a monkey sitting backwards on his head. Suddenly he stood up, for he had been sitting on the third branch of a denuded pear tree, and he invited me to stand also, which invitation I accepted. And I stood up and the name Miniharathomas crossed my lips.

If I had not known that I was mad already, I should have deemed myself so. Else why, I wondered, would this vision have come to me! My fellows on the floor, writhing in their sexual excesses, tried to drag me back down among them. But now I heard a voice — endearing, restorative — urging me to stand still and whisper one word subliminally: *Orinademtatuvirpolnarvisa!* At first, I was not sure I had heard correctly, and distraught, I bellowed, "What are you saying, whoever you are!" *Orinademtatuvirpolnarvisa!* came the command again! This time I was able to duplicate the sound and as the syllables rolled over my tongue, a grand peace descended upon me! The air around me cooled, my body became weightless, my eyes flooded with blissful tears, and I seemed to ascend from Hell and to float loosely in the glistening rainwater of a hidden stream. There was no identifying terrain, no sign in a non-existing sky by which I could gain my bearings or set my course. Ancient Mariner that I was, I just floated till everything dissolved around me, and I seemed to expire.

Upon recovering, I heard only the word *Orinademta-tuvirpolnarvisa.* I even saw the word sneaking its way through my brain. Casually I mentioned the experience to Lavinia who, afright, recognized the symptoms of revelation. In this very manner had she come to know her own Divine Fate, and although she felt she must, for this earthly time, lose me, she was sure that the revelation would ultimately lead me to the Gates of Heaven where we would most certainly be united. I had no choice, she said, but to leave the Alabaster Home for the Insane and find my way to Gilmartisa and the Being named Miniharathomas.

But how could I leave! Surely the authorities would

never let me go on such insubstantial provocation. And hadn't Lavinia explained to me that, other than the Grand Door through which each of us had entered, there was no other exit, and didn't we all know that this side of the Grand Door was impossible to find, and that even if it was found, the Windy Vestibule was guarded day and night by a mynah bird and an Egyptian cat, and that the cat watched the bird and the bird watched the cat so that whoever might pass between them interfered with their path of vision and set off their fury and their cries. And didn't we all know that no more diabolical alarm had ever been devised.

Lavinia nodded and then looked conspiringly around.

"Gather up your belongings," she whispered hoarsely.

"I need nothing but what I have with me," I said touching the flute which was tucked into my pants.

"Dearest Gregory," she said. "I know a way out. I could not bring myself to tell you about it until now. I was dishonest with you because I needed you, because I wanted you near me forever, till the end of our days should come and you and I would everlastingly hold one another in the Kingdom of Heaven. Can you ever forgive me?"

I said I could forgive her. I said even that I would forgive her.

"Give me some proof of your forgiveness and your steadfastness," she begged, "something I can treasure and hold. Something that will remind me of you always, your power, your dominion over me." Then she was silent and looked longingly at me.

"Anything, anything," I said.

She leaned towards me and touched my lips, and then she ran her fingers gently over my face, and then she dropped them sweetly on my shoulders, letting out the faintest cry. So subtly she moved her hands from my shoulders to my chest, across and down my chest to my stomach, over my stomach down to my pubic area, and finally after tracing an obvious triangle, she grabbed hold of my pudenda.

"Gregory," she whispered, "leave me this, your most precious possession. I will embolden it with gold, encrust it with gems, wear it about my neck, and when we meet in eternity, I will return it to you veiled in white gossamer as a sign that I have been faithful to you."

"Wouldn't my flute do," I urged nervously.

She grabbed harder.

"Gregory, how can you be so sportive with me at a time like this. How can you make light of the desperation of the event, of the significance of the parting, of the promise of the reunion."

"But you don't understand, Lavinia," I said trying to fight the callousness of my words with an embrace. "I need my member! I must have it with me!"

"Already you would be unfaithful to me," she said, indignation edging her voice.

She made even more desperate her hold, and I began

to feel pain.

"Folly!" I said, "I cannot think of being with anyone else now. You must know such an idea is far from my mind. I think only of *Orinademtatuvirpolnarvisa*, Gilmartisa and the Miniharathomas."

She tightened her clench till I felt if I tried to pull away, I would, without design, surrender my genitals to her.

"But when you are away from me —."

"You must trust me," I said, my words coming through biting teeth.

"Never," she said, throwing up her hands with flamboyant emphasis.

How quickly I took advantage of the moment! How, like a dervish, I spun around, fairly flying through the circles, scarcely touching the margins of the floor, Lavinia swift in pursuit of me. I did not stop to figure where I was running or when my running would end. (The damnable metaphor of it all!) I knew only that I had to keep ahead and hope that eventually I would find the exit.

Suddenly I heard a thickening scream behind me; and, unable to prevent myself from turning around, I saw the mad Lavinia standing before an open door through which I could see the outside world. She stood, daring me in her triumph at outwitting me, to retrace myself and come back to the door. She held a scimitar in her hand.

"This scimitar belonged to Alfonzo Rienzi," she

laughed, "and he undid seventy-two men with it, and if you want your freedom, Gregory, you will have to pass me and pay tribute."

My breath came graspingly, and I forced my brain to devise some plan by which I might save my member and have my freedom. The word *Orinademtatuvirpolnarvisa* joggled my brain and miraculously the answer was there.

"Yes, Lavinia," I said, "as I look at you now I wonder what good my member would be to me without you to control it. I will surrender it to you. It was my fear, my simple fear at the sacrifice that inspired such cowardly behavior."

I moved closer to Lavinia so that my actions might substantiate my words.

Lavinia stood, legs apart, the scimitar high in the air.

"How can I ever trust you again?" she cried.

There was a sharp silence and slowly I undid my trousers and showed myself to her.

"My beloved," Lavinia scarcely formed the words, "my own dear beloved."

She knelt, aiming the scimitar towards my groin as I dared move even nearer to her.

"But first, lovely Lavinia," I urged, even as I continued to approach her. "Just as you must have something to remember me by, so I wish a token from you."

"Gregory, my darling," she exclaimed with yearning delight. "Anything, anything you wish."

"One single strand of your hair —."

"A lock — a lock," she elaborated, "I will give you a lock of my hair," and she took a cluster of curls and lifted the scimitar to cut it.

"Wait — one strand, beloved, one single strand."

"But it is so difficult for me to single a strand," she said, "I would need a mirror to separate it out, and we are not allowed mirrors here, you know, lest a profound look at ourselves frightens us back to sanity again."

"Do not trouble yourself about the mirror," I said, "Let me select the strand myself, and I will use your scimitar, which belonged to Alfonzo Rienzi and with which he undid seventy-two men, to cut that strand."

"Indeed," gloried Lavinia, overcome with memory and desire, "if you select the strand, it will be the perfect one for you. But since I now hold the scimitar and am already on my knees, first let me take my tribute. Then I will close my eyes, let you cut the strand and go beyond, my ecstasy alleviating the excruciation of our parting."

"But Lavinia," said I, thanking the mysterious power of *Orinademtatuvirpolnarvisa* for my inspiration, "I must hold the strand of hair for courage during my moment of sacrifice, which you must admit, is more drastic than yours. At that moment, to gain strength, I will bind myself to you by the single hair that was your own. And also, quite practically speaking, my darling, if we reverse the procedures, need I remind you that the scimitar will be bloody, and I would not have your hair stained with blood even as testimony of our love."

"You are, my dearest, so much more schooled in the practical world than I. Is that not part of your fascination for me."

I now stood before Lavinia, who, with both hands extended, gave me the scimitar, bowing her head before me so I might select that strand of my preference.

"I will hold on to you while you cut," she said caressing my member fragilely in her hands.

The scimitar in my possession, I kissed the head I was about to deceive.

"You must let go for a moment," I implored with the feint of ardent passion. "It is a hair on the back of your head that I most desire."

And feeling her hands drop their precious holding, I spun around her, and raising the scimitar like a standard of glory, I leaped to my freedom.

CHAPTER SEVEN
Pace, Pace Mio Dio

I fled, I flew, fastening my fly, through the Alabaster Gardens and over the wall to freedom. Then, slipping the scimitar down my trouser leg to avoid its attracting comment and walking as though I had an artificial limb, I made my way to Haw-Haw's apartment.

It being the hour of his spiritual retreat, I found him hanging like a sloth from a bar which dropped from the ceiling, arms and legs wrapped around each other, eyes fixed in meditation on a small hole in the baseboards. After a mumbled greeting during which he turned himself over and over again, I raised myself carefully onto the bar, and letting the scimitar slide from my trousers, I curled myself comfortably next to him. For a moment we said nothing; then he murmured, "Due north by west, east by south, allied then alienated, but understood and remaining for always segmented friends."

After which he went limp and dropped from the bar. Seeing him motionless, I dropped beside him calling, "Haw-Haw —. Haw-Haw —." He did not answer, but suddenly I heard his enigmatic directions echoing and, picking up his body, I started moving about the apartment first north by west, then east by south, and there under the debris with which he had surrounded himself,

I saw a headstone bearing the following inscription: "Haw-Haw shall one day be united with his Melissa in the woods at the Mountain Top of Gilmartisa, in which woods he once had loved her certainly. Directions for getting to these woods can be found on the map beneath this headstone. Blessed be he, she, or they who carry my remains to that site and lay me to rest by my beloved."

An immense shiver wracked my body. It had probably been Haw-Haw who had been responsible for my revelation. It had probably been he who had alerted and inspired the Miniharathomas to reveal himself to me at this critical time in my life! And now Haw-Haw had sacrificed himself so that I might find my way to the Mountain Top of Gilmartisa and the guru Miniharathomas who had uttered the *Orinademtatuvirpolnarvisa*! At least this was all I could surmise as I lifted the headstone and found the map and prepared to sally forth bearing Haw-Haw's body as a relic before me.

But how! indeed, how now! could I get his remains out of the apartment and over the miles to our destination without arousing suspicion. Just as the thought assailed me, I saw that Haw-Haw had anticipated the problem. A mere few feet from the headstone, significantly resting in a huge cradle, lay a mummy case. So obvious a disposal unit would never be suspected. Fitting Haw-Haw's splendid corpse into it, I thrust the case over my shoulder, and, reinserting the scimitar into my trouser leg, I limped out of the apartment.

Since the journey to Gilmartisa appeared to be one

of those journeys of a million miles, I decided that I should say good-bye to my family, not merely as a matter of form, but to have one last look at them so that the image I might choose to forget would be an exact one. However, no sooner did I enter the house than my parents and my sister, who since her return from the hospital sucked convulsively on a thermometer, seeing the mummy case and believing me some harbinger of death, picked up whatever heavy and/or sharp pointed objects were at hand and sent them hurling towards me. Without even having had a chance to close the door behind me, I was forced to leave.

Unable to bear this rejection and angry with myself at my need, even for negative reasons, to identify with my family, I decided to reenter the house at all costs. Rummaging quickly through my pockets, I found, quite fortuitously, the mask I had used years before as a delivery boy. This I put on, and, hiding the mummy case and scimitar at the back of the house, I once again rang the front doorbell. There was no answer, and so I rang again; repeatedly I rang, and still there was no response. Immediately I eliminated the possibility that my family had left by the front door while I was hiding my possessions at the back door since I knew that whenever they did leave the house together they argued loudly as to which direction they should take, and, of course, I had heard no arguing. Accordingly, they had either shamed themselves into a catatonic state when they realized how cruel they had been to me or they had frightened themselves into such a state by their belief that the mummy case meant death was coming to claim them.

What a surprise was to greet me when, climbing on the roof to lower myself into the house through the bathroom skylight, I saw the three of them sitting there on the roof, each playing solitaire. I had known many evenings when we had played thus! with, interestingly enough, our circumspect innovation of exchanging hands at periodic intervals. In addition to this alteration in the game affording us a sense of competition without the brouhaha which the pressure of a normally competitive game would give rise to, it allowed us the individual maunderings of our solitary preoccupations and further provided us with regular relaxation periods from both the competition and the maunderings since, although each of us tried to play his best while he was playing his own game, he could relax and make all the errors he chose to while playing the hand of the other family members. And further, both intuitively and objectively aware of the errors that both he and the others were making, each of us took added pleasure in surely and precisely outwitting himself and his opponents. What obviously niggled me now in seeing them so casually occupied was their lack of concern at the barbarous way they had, just moments before, sent me from them. Or perhaps, in justice to them, it was their cover.

"Mother! Father! Wilma! I shouted standing on the rim of the roof and completely forgetting that they could have no idea who I was since I was wearing my mask.

"Look at me, realize me! I am about to go on a journey of a million miles, perhaps a million million miles, perhaps an endless journey as I search for my soul. Don't you want to wish me well! Don't you want to, even begrudgingly, give me your blessing!"

Wilma gnashed at the thermometer in her mouth as the three of them stared at me masked and on my knees. Simultaneously they said, "We have no idea who you are. You are masked! And though you call us by titles and names which we should recognize, we cannot recognize you."

"I will remove my mask," I said, reaching up for the meager pretense of a disguise.

"No, No, No," they uttered in unison. "We do not like penetrating the unknown. We are simple people who appreciate only what is on the surface."

"But I cannot go hidden from you forever," I wept. "Though we have had an intricately ambivalent relationship always, I cannot bear a surreptitious parting."

"If you have any feelings for us, leave us alone. What we don't know can't hurt us. And what you're about to have us discover can only cause us pain. At this point in our lives, we prefer our ignorance."

Wilma removed her thermometer and pointed it menacingly at me. Then raising it up in the air as a signal to my mother and father, she twirled it in malediction, and the three of them turned their backs on me, announcing in shrieks and screams that I would do them a great favor by leaving as swiftly and silently as I had come!

Why couldn't I have heeded their words! Why couldn't I have carried out their request! Why did I persist in making myself known to them! Leaping around them so that I faced them head on, I ripped the mask away! They groaned profoundly and each pulled at his own face as if to remove some of the invisible mask that he was wearing. Then, unable to remove any mask from his own face, each tried to remove a mask from the face of another. What a tangle of hands and arms and face pieces there was! What toning and moaning, what wailing and breast beating! So appalled was I at the grotesquerie, I could do nothing but cover my own eyes, highlighting the implicit absurdity of concealment and counter-concealment! Anguishing at their frustration in trying to tear away masks they were not wearing, they rolled about the roof, flailing at themselves and suddenly pitching themselves through the skylight. I dropped down after them, and standing above their mutilated and bloody forms, I knelt and kissed each one of them. But each kiss was a kiss of death! Precursor the mummy case was indeed! for in those brief instances of embrace, my mother, then my father, then my sister died, each having desperately swallowed a pellet of mercury from Wilma's thermometer which had smashed in her fall.

In one afternoon, I had lost Haw-Haw and my family! In one afternoon I had lost my dearest friend and most dreadful kin! How could I leave this scene! I would take my own life! With a slash of skylight glass, I would bring my own life to an end! But no sooner did this consideration enter my mind than it was dissolved by the whispered *Orinademtatuvirpolnarvisa!* Instant awareness suffused me, and I bowed my head; then raising it and my fists to the heavens I shouted the famous lines of Lear: "Pour on; I will endure!" adding as I looked down at those bloody forms which lay around me, "Requiem! Dona eis requiem!"

CHAPTER EIGHT
No Ploughshares Yet!

And then there was war!

No sooner had my family been laid to rest in a hollow behind the AUNT CAROLE, no sooner had I lifted the mummy case with Haw-Haw's body and adjusted the scimitar in my trouser leg than war was declared. I stood on the streetcorner in the midst of bewildered crowds, not sure what to do, which way to turn, how to cast my life!

How would the war interfere with my plans! What were my duties, my loyalties! Could I stop now at the threshold of my spiritual understanding, could I postpone my epiphany for war! While I explored these considerations, I sat down with Haw-Haw's mummy case beside me and stretched my leg out in front of me so as not to be castrated by the scimitar which, as it was, pressed painfully into my groin.

What a shock then, locked as I was in my meditations, to have Gretchen Allemenchen trip over me. How disquieting to see her angry face looking up at me from her sprawled position on the pavement! How disconcerting to have her utter such a diatribe of invectives!

"I am not easily brought down," she said after the word *bastard*. "And if it weren't for the mummy case which I happened to recognize as originally belonging to Semiramis, I would destroy you with the scimitar which I see protruding from your trouser leg and which, in any event, must be returned to my father if he is ever to have salvation."

"What has your father to do with it! This scimitar belonged to Alfonzo Rienzi . . . of the Medicis —."

"Indeed! But you know only part of the amazing genealogy of the weapon. So I will ask you to follow me, or better yet to link arms with me and accompany me home."

Haw-Haw, I wondered, what have you done! How much of this did you know! Even how much of it did you plan, and then, expiring, leave me to underestimate!

"No dawdling," spoke Gretchen brushing off her skirt and raising herself heavily. "Give me your arms."

She started to walk at a pace which I found, with the pull and drag of the scimitar, more than I could endure.

"You will have to endure much more before this day is over and much more before the war is done," Gretchen announced. "But , if it will help you now, you may drop my arms and I will walk more slowly and in a rhythm taught me by my father whose own biorhythms have enabled him to survive catastrophe and holocaust."

And with that, Gretchen altered her pace to what seemed like a dance beginner's two-step, the hesitant strides compensating ideally for the lag of the limp from my scimitar-splinted leg.

"The war is so sudden," I said pointlessly to Gretchen.

"Not at all," she answered. "It has been coming for years. One had only to observe!"

"Indeed?" I asked.

"Where have you been? Haven't you been following the international scene?"

I thought about the Alabaster Home for the Insane from which the real world was obscured.

"Away," I said cryptically. "Closed away."

"Hermetically sealed," Gretchen countered damagingly. "But be that as it may, you have reentered society in the midst of all the excitement. I am only amazed that my father sent me on an errand to purchase dessert at the very moment you would be sitting, leg outstretched, and trip me. But my father has such prescience." Then she quickened her stride with a new rush of enthusiasm. "We will make this war a whirlwind! We will sound the loud timbrels and dazzle the devils! You will see, Gregory — that is your name, isn't it — at least it is so written on your uniform collar. My father has been anticipating this conflict for a long time. He has said to me many times, 'Gretchen, one day I will send you to buy a dessert and on that day, war will be declared!' "

As if to corroborate what Gretchen had said, a tree uprooted crashed into the marshes through which we were now wading.

"I never did buy the dessert," she said wistfully

above the sounds of wind, lightening, and rain. "But I doubt that my father will be angry with me. He doesn't eat desserts anyhow. Perhaps he only sent me on this mission to illustrate the lunacy of life. That I could be concerned with dessert when the world was on the verge of war! Or perhaps he was using the word dessert as a euphemism for war! Oh, my wise, wise father!"

We were now waist deep in the middle of the marsh, our clothes sodden from the downpour. Unable to control myself, I asked, "How much further must we go?"

"I — I'm not sure," Gretchen said momentarily at dis-ease. "I believe I've lost my way. The storm has done it. I have never traveled home in a storm with war breaking out all around me. We might well have passed the turnoff. I admit to not remembering the marsh, but then again I have frequently forgotten familiar things, so I cannot go by that. Just bear with me. I'm hoping when we leave the marsh, I will pick up some signpost."

In the distance I now saw a series of flashes and heard the sounds of explosions.

"What's up ahead?" I asked Gretchen, fearing the answer which seemed so obvious to both of us.

"You know as well as I do," replied Gretchen, a hardness to her face. "We are approaching the war zone."

"I had no idea it was so close," I said, wanting distance.

"War is always closer than we think," Gretchen answered adversely. "I only hope my father is safe. He has merely to hear the sound of battle, and he will throw himself into the fury. He believes in war. He sees it as a purgative. He says we are always at war with ourselves so why not let it all hang out. He arranges war. He is, I believe, masterminding this one." She paused. "And though my father has not articulated the reasons clearly, he must see you as pivotal in this war. For days, he has been mumbling about the mummy case and scimitar. Then suddenly he asked me to buy dessert. And now here we are lost somewhere in the middle of a war which could very well have its origins in my father's own being. Do you not have a sense of the power of it all?"

We had traversed the marshes as she came to the end of her explanation, and as we stood in the battleground, I felt my involvement acutely. No longer was I an innocent victim of circumstances, but having the circumstances defined to me, I was now obliged to act.

"I will go no further," I said.

And with that I stumbled headlong over a large object at my feet.

"Idiot," shouted Gretchen. "Can't you see where you're going!"

I was angered. Gretchen continued to assault me.

"Can't you avoid obstacles! How are you to survive if you're so clumsy!"

But as Gretchen spoke, I became aware that the object under me was soft, that it had arms and legs, that it was, in fact, the body of a man.

"Be still," I cried. "It is you who are the idiot! Underneath me is a man, and from the sound of his moaning I would say he is a wounded man."

The body beneath me let out a wail. I looked down and saw that it was mutilated and that the rain was taking the blood in streams from his wounds.

"We cannot leave him," I said.

"There is no time to help him," argued Gretchen. She pushed the body over with her foot as I pulled myself to a standing position. "The best you can do for him is to take your scimitar and finish him off. And if you are too squeamish, I will do it for you."

"You are evil," I said.

"Now that you have spoken so rashly, what have you accomplished," Gretchen jeered at me.

"I will take this man and carry him on my back till I can find help for him."

"With the mummy case and the scimitar?" Gretchen scoffed. "You will never be able to walk a step. And there will be others. All along the road there will be wounded men! Do you intend to pick them all up! You have much to learn about the exigencies of war!"

"Listen to her," the wounded man suddenly cried out. "Save yourself. It is incredible here! I have been in wars before but never one like this. I moan as much for the violence of this war as I do for my wounds. This lady is far wiser than you. Leave me! I will not die! I have never died! I have lain on many battlefields. I have suffered all sorts of mutilations. I wouldn't know what to do if I wasn't lying on some battlefield in critical condition. Lying on one battlefield after another, I am absolved from all the other battles of my life. No one expects anything from me. And everybody is always pitying me. Why, I have been lavished over by some of the greatest physicians in the world. I have been written about in one medical journal after another. Right now, however, I'm only lightly wounded although I look much worse to an innocent like you. The doctors would hardly concern themselves with me. So you could do me a favor by just moving on, letting my condition worsen till they can't ignore me, till I become a challenge to them, and they will care for me!"

"Orlando!" shrieked Gretchen joyously.

"I wondered when you would recognize me."

"Who would have thought it! But I should have known before this! How foolish of me! You are always among the first victims, my darling. You are always so swift to throw yourself into battle. Next to my father, you are truly the bravest of the brave. And the most romantic!"

"Ha! Ha!" laughed Orlando again, obviously pleased with this tribute. "But who is this innocent you have brought to the war?"

"It is a long story," said Gretchen. "Sufficient to the day is the evil thereof!" Then she threw her arms around Orlando and whispered, "Is there time! Are there a few moments!"

Orlando stifled Gretchen's words with his lips. Pulling her to his wounded self, he embraced her. In a moment they had totally disregarded me, and, oblivious of the blood or the rain or the fury of the fray that now raged around them, they tore at their pleasures. There was no end of ingenuity to their love-making; I was both fascinated and embarrassed to watch, but in no way could I avoid their cries of ecstasy counterpointing the explosions of battle.

I waited patiently, pacing back and forth, smoking a cigarette, puffing at times unwittingly to the rhythms of their movements, even for a moment wondering how, if I ever escaped, I might use this material in a play. My speculations were, however, interrupted for, as if at the moment of his daughter's orgasmic convulsion Gretchen's father had himself been conceived, he now loomed above us on a sheer precipice of No Man's Land, dressed in war, enlarged and shadowed behind a wall of smoke-smirched glass, frantically moving artillery, soldiers, and boundary lines on a model battlefield which looked like a piece of the end of the world.

"Nothing is working," he shouted. "The General has allowed his troops to fall back, the Commander has lost most of his men, and the Brigadier —" Then, throwing one soldier after another into the air, he roared, "I can't even find him."

"Hello, Father," called Gretchen scrambling to her feet and crawling on fours up the precipice to him.

"Soon everyone will be destroyed," he screamed, his bullet-jewelled fingers flashing as he threw his arms despairingly into the air. "Already I can't find your mother."

"I'm sorry we were delayed —" Gretchen began.

"More important," demanded her father, "Did you find him! Did you find him!"

"Indeed, Father, and he carries the mummy case you were mumbling about and the scimitar of Rienzi."

"Blessed be he-he — !" exclaimed Gretchen's father, the "he-he" becoming the first two syllables of a long and gleeful and even corrosive laugh.

"It was just as you said —"

"Yes, I remember it all. I sent you to buy me a dessert because I was feeling disagreeable and wanted to plunge myself into deeper despair. But no sooner had you left than your mother unnerved me still further by insisting that environment is more important than heredity in determining the character of an offspring. I was so angered that I started the war that had been growing within me minutes before I had planned. This left me unequal to the task of balancing the forces. And I have not yet been able to remedy the situation! However, I did anticipate that if such an occurrence occurred, you would probably be at the spot where the little rat of a rose or rose of a rat would be sitting in superfluous meditations, causing all the factors to fall into place since he not only carries the scimitar but he is also of dubious heredity and antithetical environment — a mass of contradictions which satisfactorily prove neither your mother's point nor mine, but rather substantiate the cliché that there is no definable truth! Except with regard to obscurities and antitheses! Irreducible contradictions!

Mummy cases and scimitars! Or, in the normal order of things, scimitars and mummy cases! All of which supports my theory of war — what will be will be!"

Gretchen, who had been trying to console her father by a futile reaching through the smoke-smirched glass, wincingly stopped in her gropings and shifted her attention to a slight crack which had begun to work its way from the upper left-hand portion of the glass to the lower right.

"Father," she said out of context, "When I was a little girl, you used to tell me of the crack in the glass that would someday signal the decisive battle of No Man's Land. You said that on that dangerous day the crack would appear in the north by west corner of the great glass through which we all see darkly and work its way east by south, sending off tributaries as it passed through the center, which tributaries would send off others, which others would splinter into others and so forth until the entire glass would be a mass of crickly-crackly fragments which, when jarred by the Horn of Plenty sounding from the Empyrean heights of Gilmartisa would shift the central axis balancing the now and then, causing the then to erupt into battle with the now, which battle would harrowingly end our time."

"But I did not contemplate the crack for millenniums!"

"Could your calculations be wrong," Gretchen ventured, "for the crack is even now moving in its course."

Gretchen's father darted a glance at the corner Gretchen indicated. "Perhaps that is why the war is going badly. Once the great glass smashes, and we see what we see, the tensions which hold good and evil at bay will snap, and there will be a conflict so consuming as to reduce time differentials to nothing and our world to dust."

"Can he be taken seriously?" I asked Orlando.

Orlando nodded slowly. "And so too his wife who, as usual, has hidden herself away from him — and the tempestuous Gretchen. For though I lust ludicrously for her, I am not insensitive to her insidiousness, the latter aspect enhancing her attractiveness to me since you must realize by now, I myself cannot survive without the gore and stench of battle." And with that, he pulled open his jacket to reveal massive gouges in his flesh and scars in wicked patterns of neglect.

Gretchen had become aware of our conversation, and she looked askance at us.

"What are you plotting, Orlando? I have known you and known you," she cried out passionately, embracing herself, "and I know you well by now. You would have me rolling with you on battlefield after battlefield, no matter what treachery you would have to precipitate to assuage your desires."

Gretchen's father prevented Orlando from answering. "This is no time for a lover's quarrel," he expostulated, "unless such a quarrel illuminates the issues and draws the lines more clearly. But the relationship between love and passion is only an exotic trajectory to the tantalizing sexual adumbrations of war as they invert the questions of good and evil and now and then."

His sentence was punctuated with a snapping sound, and all of us directed our glances to the crack which had moved several inches further toward the center of the glass.

"May I be so bold," I ventured, "as to ask about the glass. Why is it here in the first place? What does it do? How is it inextricably involved with the ultimate end of all things in this No Man's land?"

Gretchen's father laughed disdainfully at first, then grimly, then with a sense of the folly and historic malevolence of mankind.

"It was prophesied that the fool would ask the question of the wiseman! To ask about the glass is to pose an issue akin to creation itself! Think back and you will recall that all the stories of creation speak of the division of the heavens and the earth, and/or of the seas from the sky — in fact, some division of the firmament from what is below it. Some versions then go on to create the earth if they have started with the seas or the seas if they have started with the earth. And somewhere in all this dividing and forming, separating and shaping, the stories in one way or another mention a Void. Typically the chronicles tend to dispense with the Void as if it were nothing! But the idle reality is that the Void, unseen, was also shaping Itself! And with more currency than the earth, the seas and the sky. For even as the earth, the seas and the sky thought they were crowding the Void out, It was, through an intricate process of Being and Non-Being, invisibly merging and meshing aspects of Itself with delicate intrusions, layer upon layer of nothingness, until ultimately It had realized Itself in Its Being State as a substance to which I can give only the handiest of designations by calling It glass, although I am being unconscionably clumsy by doing so.

"For you see, although this glass, so to speak, was fashioned by the same heating and cooling processes as the earth, the seas and the sky, the processes were more exaggerated in the Void as they worked more defiantly in their surreptitious ways: the Cooling Forces, which by their Nature solidified their environment, wanting to declare these positive powers by crystallizing it, while the Darkly Fiery Forces, constituted of a Destructive Nature, and preferring to work under cover, wanted to obliterate all that surrounded it. Which must make it clear to you now, Rat-Rose that you are, how the Void could continue to operate Unseen, even to the Earth, the Sea and the Sky ever being formed around it. Quite simply, the more the Positive Forces Attempted to Announce Themselves by Crystallizing, the more Swiftly did the Negative Forces attempt to Vaporize them.

"How, you are wondering, do I know all this when the matter has obviously escaped the attention of the religionists and philosophers throughout the ages who, fools that they were, seemed to be looking only when the vaporizing process was operative. Yigmarcie,

Infatato! I was only a child then, removed from other children by my recluse parents who had been removed from other children by their parents and back and back and back — even to the residual offspring of Original Sin! It was an afternoon of sunfire, and my mother had prepared a batch of cookies which she had set in the high noon heat to bake. Entrusting me, like the great King Alfred, with the responsibility of making sure the cookies did not burn, she chained me by a leash to the front of our cave so that I wouldn't be tempted to run off to play, and she cautioned me not to neglect my duties on penalty of abandonment. But no sooner had she gone than I was overcome by a moist sleep, during which I dreamed a dream.

"Loosed from my mortal coil, I found myself swallowed by a gargoyle of a serpent, among whose insides I went roaming. Pushing aside his vital organs, I was soon expelled in a violent breaking of wind, landing on a large evanescent surface which swelled and collapsed in a series of alternating whistling inhalations rendering the atmosphere cool and charming — and thunderous exhalations which flamed a heat of obscene intensity and of an odor literally of the bowels of the earth. Positive and Negative, you say! Even good and evil, I answer!"

At this point in the narrative, Gretchen's father began to cough, gasp, and choke, desperately wrenching open his collar and finally beating upon the glass which separated him from us and things from each other.

Spasmodically rallying for words, he continued: "I had proceeded — where no man should! My body — froze and steamed — the perspiration crystallizing (BrrBrr) — and melting — (WhewWhew)! Ying-yang — yang-ying — my head flipping and flopping — back and forth — forth and back! The heavy horror of it! But the more I gasped — (AchAch) — the more the freezing — (AchoooAchooo) — and the melting encased me — in a mass of glass — (Heave Ho!) — for now the hot air, more and more furiously impelled to catch up with the freezing, rose too fast, creating a whirlwind, which, cooling it, made it inoperative to sufficiently melt the cold air which clung to me. (Aye-yie-yie!) Suffocating in this armor of glass, I smashed and smashed — trying to free myself — all the time giant sounds and echoes gonging and clonging from the depths of within and the outskirts of without! (Oh, the empty, empty Void of it!) — Having voyaged to where no man should — I was to learn what no man should ever know —: the secret of impulse and expulse! — (Hiccup — ccup — ccup) — Verily, they — the sounds and the echoes said unto me, — 'Good and evil, we are — unto you! It is now — and it shall come to pass — that we shall inherit the earth! — This is the prophecy of the Void! This is — as it has been decreed! Smash! Smash! Crickle! Crackle! Even unto the end! — Thus spake Zarathustra: Arma — geedon! Arma — geedon! Blow winds blow! Fiery Furnace — Hoary Snow! Good and evil — all you know! Interjection! Violation! No amends! But down down — north by west — to south by east! Converge — diverge — submerge! — Inequity prevails! And an ill wind whines.'

"With these words, I awoke, it was years later, the cookies were burned, and my mother made good her ultimatum by unchaining me and flinging me out into the air."

"Gregory," Gretchen shouted, "Let me make quick of the story before my father is lost to us. I have heard it so many times before and can save him this terrible struggle of narration. His mother's thrust flung him back into the world he had dreamt of where he met and copulated with my mother, who had also been flung into the Void; but, in her case, by her father after she had told him of her own mother's infidelities with the Knight of the Flaming Sword, sent by God, the Holy One, Praised be He-He! to relieve the burnt-out Angel guarding the Gates to the Garden of Eden! Amen! Hail Mother of Original Sin! Then, after destroying his wife and wife's lover with the Man's Own Sword, my mother's father flung the Sword after my mother into the Void where it was snatched by the Unstructured Hand and buried in the Subterranean Envelope!

"Now the first copulation of my parents took place before they were aware of the effect of Void on Sperm and Ovaries; and, as a result of their ignorance, my brother was born a left-handed hunchback. Angered at my parents for the inconsiderate satisfaction of their lust prior to a considered understanding of the biological implications of Void on reproductive cells, my brother stole the Flaming Sword from the Subterranean Envelope, managing by a serene duplicity to leave my father's fingerprints on the Envelope. (Although my father never told me so, I suspect that my brother, in deed, cut off the tips of my father's fingers.) Then, brandishing the Flaming Sword, my brother burned his way out of the Void, and, landing in Florence, he reforged the Sword into a Scimitar so that it would not be easily identified, and then proceeded to procreate the Medici offshoot, from which line of ancestry came the infamous Alfonzo Rienzi.

"But wait! Let me anticipate your frowning concern: you are about to question how the left-handed hunchback, who started the Medici offshoot so long ago, could be my brother since I am obviously not hundreds of years old. The fact is that in the Void, because of the very freezing and melting process, time as such does not exist; it was, in fact, the very freezing and melting that whisked away the effects of the aging process so that although my brother aged and died, as did his descendants in this outer world, my mother and father remained ageless until the Void, after quandary upon quandary, finally identified my father's fingerprints on the Subterranean Envelope and expelled my parents once again into the atmosphere where they were subject to the effects of the resumption of time, depriving them of their immortality, but restoring normalcy to their reproductive systems. It was then that I was born! (An easy analogy would be that my brother came into his life in the old country; I, in the new!)

"So far as the glass behind which my father now lies suffering: At the moment of my parent's expulsion from the Void, they were engaged in one of their only happy pastimes — admiring themselves in the Shine of a Pane of Void which had not yet melted — these panes having the inviolate property while part of the Whole Void of not only holding the Image they reflected, but of course, of vaporizing it when they themselves melted. It was, in fact, the constant freezing and melting of the Held Images which whisked away the effect of the aging process from the Original. Needless to say, when the moment of Expulsion came, the Enraged Void rid itself not only of the actual presence of my parents, but also of the Pane of Itself which held their Imprisoned Images. And my parents randomly found that the piece of the Void, removed from its own environment and subject to the change of atmospheric conditions, effected two new phenomena: it did not melt, but only scorched, the Forces of Evil unscrupulously taking even more joy in smoke-smirching it and rendering it a thing through which we can see only darkly; and secondly, my parents now endlessly endured the struggle of their Imprisoned Images unrelievedly battered by the battlings of the Forces of Good and Evil, the constancy of the fragmented Pane of Void intensifying what the whole had been able to dissipate by its release mechanism of melting.

"Au Diable! A Xanadu! Even further was the trial of my parents augmented! For, being unable to clearly define their Images in the smoke-smirched glass and at the same time enduring the reflected Sufferings of these same Images, they were, as might be expected, biorhythmically clobbered by Doubt as to whether they were themselves or their Own Images!

(Author's Note: I have treated the subject of Something and Nothing of Images in my essay, "As It Is, Perhaps It Wasn't," wherein I discuss the texture of Image as it relates to Flesh and Bone, the corollary of which applies most specifically in this instance to reflection and receivership.)

"In consequence of this new kink in their lives, my parents, being pelted by the two magnetic forces converging on the Images, are wracked by cosmic schizophrenia, which, in turn, erupts in my father's unleashing wars and from which they will be released only when the scimitar you carry is returned by my father to its rightful place. For when the scimitar touches the Pane of Void as you hand it to him, it will instantly reforge itself into the Flaming Sword and dissolve the Imprisoning Pane before the Pane has had a chance to smash, at which point my father will place the Sword in the Unstructured Hand which will drop it, of course, back into the Subterranean Envelope. If these steps have been abidingly followed, the Unstructured Hand, it has been foretold, will reward my parents for their Sufferings by tossing them beyond the Void to the Empyrean Heights of Gilmartisa where all men long to go! But time is of the essence, for once the glass smashes, the chance for

Salvation will be lost. And the Harrowing will Happen."

As Gretchen finished her story, she punched and slapped at her flesh as if to exorcise from herself the spiritual struggle of her parents. I would have taken a moment to console her except that I became preoccupied with a redundancy of memory. Where before had I heard the directions with which Gretchen's father had completed his part of the narrative — north by west — east by south! My past engulfed itself in a ticker tape replay: My father had never spoken so specifically to me — nor my mother, who was more often than not, only quasi-verbal; my Aunt Carole did not believe in directions since it had always been her contention that everything was in the center, and Lavinia had considered only light and dark as *where*. Then, as Gretchen fell to the ground in the same epilepsy as her father and the imminence of death became palpable, I thought of Haw-Haw lying in the mummy case! Yes, indeed, it was he! or rather it had been he who had given me those same directions in leading me to the headstone in his apartment! Quickly I pulled the map from my pocket and noticed that it did not so much indicate directions as show barbed wire enclosures of blackened blood-spattered space and emptiness! Could there be some connection between the death and *liebestod* of Haw-Haw and the Armageddon of No Man's Land which Gretchen's father had prophesied! I remembered Gretchen's reference to the Gilmartisian Heights! Had I been led to this monstrous bloodbath simply to pass through hell to heaven!

My penumbrations were interrupted as Gretchen stopped her groveling and directed her venom at me.

"It is you!" she screamed. "Rat-Rose that you are! It is the impulses which distinguish your own personality which are animating the good and evil powers being held at bay behind the splintering glass. You have only to stand there, and their struggle is manifold! Orlando! Orlando!" she cried, baring her breast, "we have brought the enemy into our midst! My father has been deceived! Somehow all the messages have gotten crossed! Or else — indeed! Of course — they have been deliberately intercepted and interfered with by the supernal influences unleashed by my long-lost-left-handed-hunchback of a brother, who, fearing what the return of the Sword might mean for his shade has, from his place in the nether world, presaged this apocalypse by maneuvering the scimitar to fall into the only hands which, returning it, could at once destroy all those who might profit by its return! Oh! Oh! Oh why did we not see how my brother had engineered my father's evil self to blind his ying to the clues!" Then, pointing to me, "We must eliminate this Rat of a Rose, my brother's emissary!"

"But I don't even know your brother," I reasoned.

"One does not have to know my brother to serve him," Gretchen answered with violent obscurity. "He is containing."

I stood firm! I looked about! Gretchen was lifting

herself to her knees. Her father and/or his reflected image were crawling up the wall of the Pane of Void! Orlando was adjusting his trousers, for, as soon as he had seen Gretchen in spasms on the ground, he had surged with sexual excitement! I looked up! I looked down! Still no idea for escape nor plan of action suggested itself. There was a new snap of glass and the north by west to south by east crack splintered, intersecting itself by a south by west to north by east crack which as it crossed, caused the two diagonals to split again into two additional diagonals, the glass now divided into eight sections. My memory was prodded! This was it! With stunning creative recognition, I remembered Aunt Carole's affinity for the figure eight. Those intransigent eights she would trace in the air to restore harmony! Balanced as they were so perfectly! Turned likewise top and bottom! Similarly opposite! If, as Gretchen said, I was, by merely standing neutral, animating the forces of good and evil, perhaps I could by turning myself around in the equal halves of an eight, reverse the polarity of the forces, and, in so doing, create some combination in the design of diagonals that might neutralize the smashings and save me! It was certainly worth a try!

I did my deed of daring-do, apparently only causing a holding pattern just as the glass split into a mere sixteenths. But I had yet to reverse the process. I was immediately and again inspired, this time by Aunt Carole's childhood admonition during the Indian head-dress burning — "Don't ever give up! It is only when thou giveth up that Thou truly loseth." Now as I traced the eights, I expanded the coverage area by swirling my arms in an ever-widening balloon, an improvisation which seemed to me to have an arch pertinency. That was enough to do it! The splintering, now redirected, occurred in circles, a holy configuration of diagonals and curves causing a remission in the disaster process. One more balletic turn and the scoops fixed and supported the diagonals like the splendid structure of a Gothic window.

However, this stasis was only temporary. Gretchen, taking advantage of the halt and enlisting Orlando's help with a vulgar battle cry, lunged at me trying to wrest the scimitar from my possession and destroy me with it. Gruntingly, the three of us twisted into each other, I straining arms against breasts and knees against belly till I felt blood and gall mix and pound my veins and arteries to bursting! Then just as my brain was about to blacken, I saw, through Gretchen's armpit, in the center of the holy pattern now holding the smoke-smirched glass together, a glorious roseate of light framing a silhouette which I recognized as that of the Minihara-thomas wrapped in sheep's wool, the monkey sitting backwards on his head. He extended his arms to me as the incisive pronouncement of the Horn of Plenty of which Gretchen had spoken sounded from the glittering heights of the Mountain Top of Gilmartisa! Instantly was the hold of Gretchen and Orlando released! And instantly also with the sounding of that Horn of Plenty did the mummy case of Semiramis open and did Haw-Haw step out! (How I wondered whether he had ever died or whether, actor that he was, he had only feigned death!) With his superb art of mime, he signaled me to be careful not to let the scimitar get into the hands of any of the Allemenchens, for they were of a doomed race who, despite and because of their aspirations, could never be trusted, but to thrust the scimitar speedily and hardly into the earth!

This I did, only to see the splintered Void disintegrate and the Unstructured Hand emerge to fetch and return the Sword to the Subterranean Envelope. At which moment, the monkey leaped from the head of the Mini-harathomas, and, scrambling to the model battlefield, laid it waste. This microcosmic destruction triggered a macrocosmic eruption. Monkeys and Men, thrust into battle from topside and hindside, from forward and backward, mangled one another while Gretchen's father raged conflicting orders first to one, then to the other. The glitters from the Gilmartisian Heights spun into balls of flame and rained down, igniting fire upon fire whose crackly-crickly sound, augmented by the crickly-crackly crunch of the disintegrating Wall of Void, resulted in an ultra-high frequency pitch of such piercing intensity as to split eardrums and distort brainwaves. When I thought I could bear the multimedia blitz no longer, a dove shaped itself from the rising vapors of battle. (She it was, the metamorphosized Semiramis who, wondrous tale tells us, was in this manner transmogrified at her life's end.) The dove, smiling and fluttering her wings, seductively encouraged Haw-Haw and me to mount her as she lifted us high above this *Welteruntergang*! With an Orpheusian curiosity, I turned my head and saw in the furnace below me a figure of wens and warts (later identified as Gretchen's mother) rise up from the cross-hatch of debris and fling herself with a wail of a whine into the arms of her husband who marched with her into the engulfing holocaust, stalwartly stepping over Orlando and Gretchen, whose lusts, detonated by this bountiful bombardment, had enjoined them to set their passions free.

CHAPTER NINE
The Dawn Birds Sing
and Then Some

Dawn! Dawn! Dawn! It was dawn! dawn! dawn!
On the Mountain Tops of Gilmartisa as the Dove of
Semiramis with its precious burden of Haw-Haw and
me sailed onto a cloud-wrapped crag jutting out over a
cloud-draped stream in the middle of which, cushioned
on a cloud, floated the gentle Miniharathomas with the
monkey returned and once again sitting backwards on
his head. His white hair fell over his face, covering most
of it, pulled away from only his smile like a curtain
framing a proscenium; below his smile, and having
artfully shed his sheep's wool cloak in the heat of the
battle below, he was now swathed in a fabric (perhaps
essence would be a more accurate term) whose texture
and color changed with each tint of light patterning it.
His imperceptible movements seemed determined from
outside his will — for he waved or trembled or shivered
or swayed according to the subtlest shift of breeze. He
had, in truth, so given himself over to the forces of nature
that he had become a part of them.

He did not speak, but only stared at us with a smile,
a smile which, we were to learn, served as his eyes and

tongue as well, and soon Haw-Haw and I realized that we too were smiling although our smiles seemed to carry more meaning for the Miniharathomas than they did for us. The question which posed itself to me was whether I should speak or wait until I was spoken to. Finally, with great courage, I rolled out the word *Orinademtatuvirpolnarvisa*. As the last syllable left my lips, the smile of the Miniharathomas rippled, revealing the shape of the word appreciatively in reply, the image of the consonant and vowel patterns oscillating in such exacting a random pattern as to create the echo of speech without its utterance. As this unearthly reverberation soared in a glorious harmonic, the dove slipped out from under Haw-Haw and me (leaving us slightly floating) and sailed over towards the Miniharathomas where, after what appeared to be a genuflection — or as near to a genuflection as can be managed by a dove — it rose up onto the shoulder of the monkey and cajolingly cooed *Orinademtatuvirpolnarvisa*.

This cooing of the *Orinademtatuvirpolnarvisa* set up a trail of breath much like that pictured leaving the pursed lips of Zephyr in the Botticelli "Birth of Venus," and onto this train of air, apparently materializing from the cooing lips of the dove, danced seventeen golden gnats, attached to one another by a silver thread. They came toward us with a bizarre elegance tweeting a fragile chant, the text of which was barely audible. Only after countless repetitions was I able to make out the story of the song which recounted the defection of the gnats from

Egypt at the time of the third Plague and of the asylum which the earlier reincarnated Miniharathomas had offered them from the Wrath of God. The song went on to praise the way Miniharathomas, the Elder, had assuaged God, and the way God had then showed His contrition by golding the gnats and giving them for messengers to the Miniharathomas. This "Song of the Golden Gnats" (which I have included in my anthology, *Prehistoric Folklore of the Diptera Order*) ends with an anthem-like coda extolling Moses and his uncircumcised lips in terms of the categorical imperative.

With the last note of the Song, the trail of breath from the Dove evaporated. It was now obvious how completely the performance by the Golden Gnats had delighted the Miniharathomas, for his smile broke and closed, broke and closed, his lips piping a pip-pip-pip sound of applause, the wee wisps of air from the delicate ovation furnishing a new floor of air on which the gnats could remain afloat without exerting any effort of their own. Then flushed by the pleasure they had brought the Miniharathomas, the Golden Gnats most gracefully inclined their heads and, still remaining joined by the silver thread, they danced towards him and strung themselves zig-zag about his neck.

A mysterious impulse now urged me to chance the *Orinademtatuvirpolnarvisa* again, this time even more boldly and, by my so doing, I set a new sequence of events into happening. The Miniharathomas once more shaped the word in reply, only this time his smile carried a slight teasing to it. The dove lifted itself off the shoulder of the monkey and began to circle the Miniharathomas, the currents of air now causing him to sway from side to side. This movement provoked a movement of the stream under him, the spray of which rose like a curtain between the Miniharathomas and Haw-Haw and me. The more speedily the dove circled, the more active became the movement of the waters and the more dense the spray; it was now impossible to see the Miniharathomas, the monkey or the dove, so heavy was the curtain of spray, but both Haw-Haw and I were aware of the activity behind the curtain, that same kind of rustling and bumping one hears when scenery is being moved during a blackout at a theatre.

Needless to say, Haw-Haw and I were struck by the spray, but we were not being wetted. Indeed, wherever the waters touched us, a speckle of film formed till we were encased in a transparency which warmed and coddled us. So sensually were we soothed by the coddle that I felt immediate sexual arousals, but none such as I had ever experienced before, for my arousals were simultaneously those of the lover and the beloved. I swooped down upon myself, being at the same instant the penis-prober and the receptacle of my own probing, my chest pressing the systemic hardness against my own breasts which heaved voluptuously to receive this other self. My lips, all lust, opened against the full sweetness of my own passionate other lips, teeth against teeth, tongues entangled. Arms embraced the torsi of this divided self and legs grappled around each other, strong with the surging intensity of giving and holding. The rhythms of intercourse exquisitely adjusted themselves with rubato pulsings, prolonging the crescendo fulfillment, enlarging the envelopment, drawing with double tantalizing tautness the tightening of the orgasmic coil. I gasped, I cried out, I moaned and grunted as I felt myself edging, edging over a divine chasm from which emanations of ecstatic swellings rose with a swift and fierce frequency until no muscle nor nerve nor single space of double flesh was able to withstand the stabbing completeness of the assault and so, consequently, tore at their parts with crazed abandon, spasms and waves rocking and undulating in tandem climax.

"Oh, ah, eee, uh — yow!" shrieked Haw-Haw in tenor, alto, soprano, and bass, sounding the grand Amen of every lover's yelp, quadrupling my joy by his own double orgy as the curtain of spray spurted, splashed and finally subsided, revealing a scene of melody and paradise, ablaze with a blue-gold glow filtering from the figure of the Miniharathomas, now elevated on a pillar of fountaining sea-foam, atop which was a seat of crystals set in a bower of birds, bees and flowers.

The birds were dawn birds. Found only in these Gilmartisian heights, they are seven-winged, each wing replicating in color one of the ribbons of the rainbow, and twelve-footed, each foot having from one to twelve toes according to the stage of its development. A fully developed dawn bird can have as many as one hundred and forty-four toes unless he has lost one or two (which most dawn birds do since the tensile strength of dawn birds' toes is low and they snap easily.) Barring such loss, it is possible for dawn birds to travel as much as twenty times faster on foot than they do in the air (the propelling power of wings and feet being almost equal). The outlandish speed differential sometimes causes dawn birds to topple and spin pinwheel fashion at moments of lift-off (a more obvious reason for the preponderance of lost dawn birds' toes). As a matter of fact, it is not infrequent to see dawn birds choose to go into flight by deliberately toppling and spinning, building their take-off currents by the bursts of air they create revolving.

The bees too were a naturalist's dream, having extended sucking, excretory, and procreating organs, which made them translucently easy for study. Were it not for their curled antennae (alive with a mustard colored symbiotic plant life), they looked almost like the smallest winged baboons. These wings, unlike the festive wings of the dawn birds, were a pale cloud-grey which offered the gentlest background, when fully spread, for the mustard-colored plant life on the antennae.

Regarding the melody of this paradise: The song of the dawn birds was constant, and, although slightly atonal, it resolved itself with metronomic frequency into a rhapsodic gigue — (this musical contrivance also caused dawn-bird toe loss since the birds, inspired by their own song, would periodically leap into outrageously erogenous dances). Nor was the bee song the simple buzz that we identify with our species of common bee, but rather it was a scooping tessitura which counterpointed and harmonized with the song of the dawn birds, more often than not with glissando speed and rapturous lilt. The breeze, of course, carried its own elusive vibrations — sometimes pantingly exotic — sometimes organically organ-like, and I believe truly the source of the toning om *Orinademtatuvirpolnarvisa.*

Of the flowers which abounded in this Garden of Gardens, what can be said but that they responded in their own irreducible way to the paradisiacal pitch of the music, swaying and nodding and playing prankishly with puffs of perfumed pollen deliciously intoxicating themselves into producing bloom upon bloom of blossoming hybrid bouquets, which forever shifted their hues.

And here we were, Haw-Haw and I, stunned pilgrims in this Holy Shrine, the Miniharathomas smiling down on us, his smile encouraging us to look more closely at ourselves. This we did, only to see that the transparent film which had been responsible for our sexual activities had further dissolved the clothes which we had been wearing and that the sexually dual experiences we had been undergoing had indeed a newly-developed physiological basis.

Man and Woman, Created He them, the Lord God, the Holy One, Praised be He! Created He them to be as One to the Other! Created He them to Mate and Propagate! Created He them to be as Companions, the

One to the Other! Created He them to be as a Signpost, as a Doorpost, the One to the Other! To be as Frontlets For Their Eyes, the One to the Other! To Separate and Come Together, the One to the Other, to Love and Be as One, the One to the Other! But Yea! now they were not as the One to the Other! They, who were One in the Sight of the Miniharathomas, had, indeed, been transformed by that Sight so that they were! Behold Them! Truly One!

So it was in Amazement that we looked upon ourselves, Haw-Haw and I, and each of us was astounded by what had come about and upon His Own Body. For indeed, the Body was well-nigh changed, revealing swells and curves, projections, crevices and folds, muscles and orifices — all those of male and all those of female together in conglomerate and as One!

To celebrate our transformation, the dawn birds and the bees, the gnats and the organ breeze offered hallos and jolly-goods in rounds, hymns, anthems, and jingles.

The Miniharathomas sensed our discomfiture: his smile grew benign and suddenly the echo of *Orinademta-tuvirpolnarvisa* was heard, and with it, what appeared to be a translation, and beyond that a ramification, a commentary, a Mishna and Gemara: "Love everlasting, the One for the Other, love which we need, the One from the Other — love which is One — done! Each, not two — woebetide! woebegone! for they are unto conflict — appeasing and releasing, releasing and appeasing, without cause, but selfishly! Do you not see or feel what cannot be two! No need for consultation, nor persuasion, nor encounter, nor deception! but the searching ends and there is only finding! The finding binding! The binding finding! Found! And unto each of you, there is the other — engaged by flesh, surrounding itself with its own desires, satisfying from within by what is no longer without — nor without the within! Having won what it had not — no longer not having what it must win! Entirely complete when it is singly two, rather than twice one, perhaps even a parallelogram! Agreement satisfies! Remedies rescind recoil! Angels no longer lament but laud! laud! laud! Acquiring new rights at their own behest! Without abstinence! With only overload! Overload of overlove enhancing! Benighted and extreme! Gently, gently, benighted and extreme!"

The music of the hallos and jolly-goods rose and made its way in fine and thinning curves back to its origin, sending out circles of sounds which linked with one another in binomial frolic. I looked at Haw-Haw whose usually grave aspect seemed now quite madcap.

"Once when I was a little little boy of the streets," he said with a blithering glint of rampant recollection, "I remember ambling through an alley way, kicking up stones and smashing tin cans beneath my tread. It was evening and from kitchen window after kitchen window came the corned beef and cabbage sounds of pots and pans mixed with the alluvial voices of husbands, wives, and children. Feeling suddenly faint, I halted my way, and leaning against a garbage pail, appropriately lapsed into pondering the commonplace. 'Dear God,' said I, 'Let me be a walrus, an aardvark, a minimum essential, but let me not be a donkey!' "

Haw-Haw stopped speaking, and touching himself significantly, he mapped out the terrain of his altered form, cupping his hands in some new places, closing and opening his fingers around others, smoothing and petting, tapping and snapping. Such was the eloquence of his gestures that this reconciliation of his parts spoke intrinsically of the vagrant answer to his child's prayer, of the pandering relationships of men and women, of sexual adversities and adverse sexualities. Then, extending his arms in worshipful adoration, he fell upon his knees, and without attempting to control his passions, spoke these words: "*Orinademtatuvirpolnarvisa*! I, who was not, AM! I, who AM, will be! No further ado and Always Complete! For now I understand, having put away childish things and become, in Thy Sight, Oh Mini-Mini-harathomas, the perfect thing! a single cell multiplied twice again in its singleness!"

I wish I could have agreed! But I felt unfamiliar with my changes. I could not somehow identify as readily with my second self as Haw-Haw had with his. Almost in answer to my own misgivings, Haw-Haw went on!

"She who was gone is come again to me! We are now as we could only have hoped to be! Arresting ourselves in Each Other and Resting Surely There Together, no more wear, no more tear! For I know you now, my Melissa! I am aroused now within myself by the You You are and the I who I am! All things retaining!

All things sustaining!"

And with that Haw-Haw pressed his hands around his/her breasts and sighed and wept! How he did weep with an incredible joy!

"*Orinademtatuvirpolnarvisa*! My failure has again triumphed! As Melissa was gone, so she has returned unto me! Eurydice! My long sojourn even unto the gates of Erebus has led me to her! As she was, so she will be even more so in me! For I am now she! And she the very I of me! Ergo! Melissa and Haw-Haw are now truly conjoined!"

Haw-Haw went on and on, praising this transformation, conjuring up all sorts of dialogues and encounters with his beloved Melissa who, he was convinced, was this newly developed feminine form of himself. I respected Haw-Haw too much not to believe him. I judged he knew what he was feeling and what he was saying. And anyhow I thought, if he was so happy, who was I to interfere! After all he had vowed to be reunited with Melissa, and he had gone to the trouble of dying to accomplish this end; for, despite my wanting to believe that his death was only the most divine of his performances, I remain fully convinced that he had been dead when I put him into Semiramis' coffin and that he had arisen at her behest at that moment of the Armageddon. All I could say to myself, though I didn't dare even think a word of it aloud was, So be it, Haw-Haw, and I'm glad for you, but it just seems to be a bit depriving. To me, it seems to take the tickle out of things. The whole arrangement is predicated on the premise of the constancy of love. And, of course, it is the inconstancy of love that obviates the boredom and replenishes the bloom. (I make much of this in my *Gilmartisian Oratoria*, Opus 0–4, the only musical work I have composed, but one which joined the standard repertory of choral groups all over the world almost immediately after its notorious — what a paltry word to use considering the aberrational events of that unholy night! — first Paris performance. Utilizing the songs of the dawn birds, the bees and the soughing wind as a musical demography, the text deals with the virtues of having two separate sexes as opposed to the single unit set-up. It is in the *furioso* duet for bass and counter-tenor, "Arrest me, Mother, I shall be ne'er again," that the voices tangle ribaldly with the matter as they banteringly toss into the air the lines, "There is less to constancy than rightly meets the eye, for 'Tis the searching makes the bedding more the wry." But the full joy of the word play comes with the ornamentations as "wry bedding" bucks "constant searching," and the "inconstancy of constant searching" titillates the "wryness of the bedding eye.")

Be all that as it may, it was certainly the wryness of the Miniharathomas' inner eye that was more than a little chagrined at perceiving my thoughts on the matter. For even as Haw-Haw was at his most feverish in his avowals to his other self and the Miniharathomas, I sensed in that most revealing of smiles a change which I knew to be inspired by his displeasure with the withholding of myself from his gift. No longer was it charmingly satisfied; rather it was beginning to twist, narrowing itself till the lips were barely distinguishable. Then, almost convulsively, the lips began to move much in the manner of the lips of someone trying to hold back a sneeze or to prevent himself from weeping or perhaps more accurately trying to do both even while trying to suppress an anger rising in him.

Concomitant with the lip change was a change in the Gilmartisian setting. All the blue-gold glow fogged into grey-bronze, the full-blown flowers drooped, the dawn birds dirged, the bees droned as their protruding organs shrank, the breeze wailed, and the gnats flattened around the neck of the Miniharathomas as if they had been swatted. The spurting fountain which had held up the crystal seat subsided, the very waters drying up, and the crystals clotting into clumps as of muddied snow.

And then a change took place in the Miniharathomas himself. The fabric of his garments, which I better described as a substance, blurred, revealing his skeleton beneath — a kind of Divine X-Ray of willow weeds — which weeds then seemed to waft themselves away, leaving only his head held up by the flattened gnats. Just as dramatically, the dove turned its back on us. And finally, and most appallingly, the white hair of Miniharathomas fell in outlandish array over his lips and all of Gilmartisa was awesomely dark.

Here there is a terrible lacuna in my memory. As if the darkness in Gilmartisa was also a darkness in my mind, as if my own life had been interrupted by the Miniharathomas' withdrawal of himself. Without his presence, nothing was well managed; and, though I know that there was no spite intended in the catastrophe that followed and that every effort was made by the minions of the Miniharathomas to restore me properly to my former self before they released me as a creature fallen from Grace, they made capital errors in the process. They simply removed the right things and left the wrong things, so that when I did come to, after having been flung out of Gilmartisa to avoid the Miniharathomas' ever having to face his failure, it was to land as a wretched whore in a brothel in Paris with Georgette Playel looking down at me whispering, "You ave ad a deefeecult time, ma chérie, un temps tres deefeecile."

PART THREE

Le Jour de
Gloire est Arrivé

CHAPTER TEN

The Bugs in the Bed Would Die, Would that I!

I am a fastidious man! I wash my hands each time many times and then wash the spigot handles so that when my washed hands turn off the spigot, they will not be contaminated by any residuals from the unwashed hands which had turned it on. I will not eat in restaurants nor sleep in hotels for obvious and respective reasons. It is only the fiercest discipline that allows me to use the seats in public vehicles, theaters or concert halls, and only the most importunate erotic urgings that sear from my brain the severe misapprehensions that assail me at moments of sexual participation.

Imagine then the frenzy that beset me on finding myself in a brothel bed! And the miasmic revulsion that undulated through me as I realized to what purpose I might be lying on these particular sheets. No sooner had I opened my eyes than I closed them, fiercely hoping to eviscerate from my thinking any taunt of the truth. But the heavily painted face of Georgette insinuated itself even into this forced darkness, and I tried not to consider whether in my unconscious state, I had already been used to satisfy the lust of some corpulent oaf.

"Let me die, let me die, let me die," were the words sponged from my soul to my inner ear. "Dear God and/ or Miniharathomas whom in my ignorance and/or innocence I may have offended — Dear Haw-Haw, if you have any influence in whatever dead/alive, male/female form you are! Dear Aunt Carole or Long Lost Samuel Kitchelpop — please any one of you surreal ectoplasms who can put in a good word for me with the Grim Reaper — know how I long to be cut down by that Scythe!"

I lay still in bed, trying to convince myself that no movement might somehow keep me inviolate, that if I withdrew inside my motionlessness, I might escape contamination.

"Ma pauvre petite," said Georgette, " you ave not known me for days and days. I ave watched ovaire you wiz all my dealoojonz. I ave short-changed my customaires all zee owaires of zee day and night and I ave rushed vite vite to you. Pleeze ma pauvre petite, opein youaire eyeze and regardes-moi."

The voice was fragile and concerned, but I could not bear acknowledging it. To do so would mean to face the extremity of my situation and this was an anathema to me. As is I could not ascertain whether there were bugs in the bed, but their mere physical absence seemed of little significance to my outraged self which felt besieged by them. I knew that they and all the wormy germs from all the copulating occupants of the room were swarming over me with gluttonous abandon and that they were penetrating my skin even unto the marrow of my bones, my blood stream, my fainting heart. I conjured images of every scrofulous face, every leprous lip with which, in my most destructive imagination, I might ever have been touched. I tore in my guts with convulsions of volcanic proportions.

"You do not like eet — to be haire — you weel not opein youaire preety blue eyze, you weel not wheespaire to Georgette that you aire grateful to me for all I ave done. For I ave done much for you. I ave sacreeficed much for you in zee long owaiares seence I ave found you."

A denser nausea seeped through me! Where had Georgette found me! What worse circumstances had I been in! To what other degradations had I been subjected since Gilmartisa had gone dark. I knew I must open my eyes, bolster my will. I must hear her out.

"Forgive me," I whispered in a voice that fought its own utterances. "It is all strange to me. I have lost memory. I have been violated in the most unspeakable ways, not being what I appear to be. I am almost incapable of civility, and I fear intricately all that you are about to recount to me."

"We aire none uv us what we appaire to be, ma chérie. In my work, c'est tout deception. Eef you only knew how I — moi-même — suffaire — ach! you must not be led to theenk my painted face does not hide une vérité terrible! Eef I wash away zee colaire — what you would see would not make you aapppeee! I couvaire my sins wiz zee rouge and zee powdaire and zee —" The tears watered Georgette's eyes, and she folded her hands over her face and sobbed. "You aire zee only one to whom I opain my heart, for I know we aire sistaires souffrantes, and zat givain ze choyce — mais qui! — who in zis impossible world is evaire givain ze choyce!

"I am une enfant of zee devil? Ma mère and mon père — zay waire two people who did not caire about me! Zey leeve for zemselves — not evain for each ozaire — zey both love themselves to zee point of murdaire. Ah oui! One day mon père, he eez so jealous zat my mothaire love herself more zan she love heem — he slice her throat — he slice zee throat of my mothaire across zee neck — zen he dissapaire — and I confeze to you — I tell you, mon ange, — I fear evairy man who take me in heez arms—. Eet eez my torture! Eet eez my penance for my life — I say peut-être zis man eez mon père disguised or peut-être he eez a friend de mon père who he az sent — or a brothaire unknown to me — and souvent — I do not ave zee control of myself — so angry I am zat I cannot have peace and zat evairyzing eez for me — how you say — zeeg-zag — zat I theenk — ach! mon ange — I cannot tell you what I theenk, but eet eez vairy terrible — for I theenk — often I theenk I will grap zee orgain of my customaire and pull it away — pull it off uv heeze body in mon estrange-ment . . ."

Memories of Lavinia superimposed themselves on Georgette as she went on recounting her story with increased passion.

"But zen, ma chérie — I find you — and you ave done what I ave only been afraid of doing! I deed not believe eet! C'est incroyable, I say! Mais eet eez so! The proof eez thaire in youaire hands when I find you wiz all zee rats as I walk by zee garbage dump on my way chez-moi!"

I could not anticipate the absoluteness of the rest of her narrative, but I felt myself, without daring to reason why, on the point of annihilation.

"Eet eez so — clutched een youaire fingaires eez zees leetle bag — and when I bring you back haire — in my arms comme un enfant — I opain zee bag — and I find zees!"

She opened the bag and there lay the critical part of my other self, that distinguishing organ which the minions of the Miniharathomas, finding left over when they had reassembled me, had packaged for me and flung with me out of Gilmartisa.

"And eet eez then I know we aire seestaires souffrantes — and I ask myself — pourqoui — what az made yeu zo désespéré to do zees zing uv which I ave only dreamed!"

"No, No, Georgette," I wanted to say. "You do not understand — I ave not done zis thing. It az been done to me! What you have thaire is my own —" But I could not say the words. I could not bring myself to such an admission, and I feared for myself should Georgette learn that in truth I was or had been a man.

"I must not ask —" Georgette said. "Eet ees too much of youaire heart! I trezpass too soon. You ave barely awakened. Someday you weel teel me. Mais — pour maintenant — I shall take caire uv you! You weel not ave to do anyzing! You will rest, ma chérie —"

My heart now unhinged, I nodded my head as if in gratitude for what she was saying and then, pretending to drift off to sleep, I felt the bed respond to Georgette's rising, and I slit open my eyes to see her gently place the little bag in the dresser drawer. Then I watched her as she looked at herself in the mirror, took a fluff from a powder box and touched her face, fingered some rouge onto her lips and quietly left the room.

I tossed agonizingly, wondering why the gods had led me to such a crossroads and what I could possibly do with the wretched me that seemed to persist. I saw no course of action; perhaps because I eschewed the thought of life itself. From the next room I heard Georgette's professional laughter, then the grunting monosyllables of a male voice, the accelerated rhythmics of the bed-springs, and illiterate expelling of the archetypal ah, oo, ugh, eee! and then a swift silence.

To try to divert myself from the utter vulgarity of it all, I resorted to what had been a failproof trick of mine developed when, early on, I had first worked to strengthen my stringent powers of concentration. The effort consisted of punching hole after hole in an unwanted stream of consciousness to create in the brain's kaleidoscopic imagery black areas as close to circular as possible till the holes merged to form a *tabula rasa* upon which I could begin a new construct. However, my rank imagination now resisted my hole punching, and I lay helplessly diseased by the loathsome stimuli with which I was being assaulted. But even as I meditated on my lot, I mercifully drifted off to sleep, and when I looked about me again, what little natural light had been in the room was gone, and only a naked bulb gave a yellow cast to Georgette who, once again, sat over me.

"You aire awake," she said, "you aire recovering. I can tell. Eet eez the one leetle plejaire now een my life. To ave a seestaire weez me. Ma chérie, eet as been so lonely for me, and now —" She threw her arms up and then clasped the air with her hands.

Whether it was the fancy of her gesture or the quick glimpse the catching of the air gave me once more of Gilmartisa, I suddenly sat up in bed, momentarily disoriented by the flow of hair which now touched my shoulders and the weight of breasts which embarrassed me. I pulled up the blanket and Georgette responded with a spray of laughter.

"Ma chérie — oh, ma chérie — you need not covaire youairezelf — we aire seestaires —" and she leaned forward and pulled the blanket aside. "Youaire beautiful — you should not be ashamed. "And then she drew my breasts to her lips and kissed them.

I swept the covers off and got out of the bed, sensing a whole new balance to my body. Georgette, believing I was shaky from my stupor, immediately thrust her arm under mine to offer me assistance.

"I ave une jolie robe for you," she offered and seeing that I could manage to stand, she rushed to the closet and pulled from it a flowered silk wraparound which I quickly drew on. "Violà, c'est mieux!" she delighted.

The next hour was taken up with a delirious toilette as Georgette led me through a perfumed bath and body powdering, then helped me dress with airy underthings, a silken shirt blouse and a wisp of a pink-side-slit skirt, each new addition to my apparel bringing gleeful appreciation from her. The dressing process seemed to give me new breath so that by the time I stood in front of the full-length mirror, I felt strong enough to agree to Georgette's suggestion that we go to a bistro to celebrate our sisterhood with a bottle of wine. As Georgette and I entered the small overcrowded cellar, she suddenly turned to me: "Youaire name? — comment tu t'appelles? —" "Gregory," was about to spring to my lips — but the moment's hesitation in which I knew I must drive the masculine appellation back caused Georgette consternation. "You ave forgotten youaire name — mais — non! ave no fear. I find you one —." Then she took a deep meditative inhale —. "Je le sais! C'est parfait! I call you — comme une belle fleur — la Rose!"

CHAPTER ELEVEN
La Vie en Rose

My life as Rose lasted through only one monthly cycle, just time enough for me, however, to conceive a child, fathered by Zeus, disguised for all his earthly pleasures as the dashing Marquis de Connaissance. The child, much like Bacchus, had for its own welfare to be removed from me prior to the further physiological changes I was destined to undergo, but from hearsay, I have been able to determine that it was, indeed, a man-child, and that, to prevent his wife Hera from taking vengeance on the fetus, Zeus, this time instead of using his own side as surrogate womb, divided the gestation period (by means of dizzying sleight-of-hand obstetrics) among the Muses, each of whom concealed the child for a month, and then all of whom, in amazing concert, so enchanted Hera with birthing songs as to make her look kindly upon the boy and accept him as a gift, calling him Many-Mothered and bestowing him with godly status.

However, as must be obvious, no summary of such a month could convey this time of joy, trial, and surprise. Georgette was a perfect darling, feeding me broth and honey, and building in me a feminine mystique which allowed me to walk the streets of Paris with pride, even with a certain dégagé. We were indeed sisters, reveling in each other's faults and sympathizing and empathizing with all our palpitations and frustrations. In turn, I was an eye opener for Georgette, guiding her from museum to museum, from theatre to theatre, from concert to concert — sometimes to three, four or even five events in a single day, illuminating for her the stresses, balances, insights and inspirations, the technical skills and explosive inventions of great art. I was enthusiast and teacher, fillip and frankincense.

Indeed, it was at a tiny Musée on the Rue des Arts where an exquisite exhibition of Greek artifacts and miniature sculptures was being displayed that I was tried by the Lord of the gods Himself. The museum had evening hours on the third Thursday of the second, fifth, seventh, ninth and tenth months of the year! And Georgette and I had the good fortune to reach its doors at that transparent twilight-of-the-gods on a breathless May night. I felt the suspense of miracle even as I approached the garden, and, by the time I had stepped over the threshold, I knew I would not leave the premises untouched in a way known to few men or even women, for that matter.

The display case in which the Zeus sculpture appeared was off to the side of the last main exhibition room, in a kind of cul-de-sac, and Georgette, fatigué, decided to relax on a banquette in the larger salon. While I lingered on alone, the light from the floriated stained glass window settled almost fragrantly on the glass case, surrounding the tiny bronze piece in a whimsy of sustained transience. In fact the piece, even on first glance, seemed to have a life of its own, emanating a glow so recherché that it obliterated the source, and, for an instant, the Zeus appeared displayed by its own aura. It was at such a moment that the corpus of the Marquis was beside me, or rather his shadow fell over me. In all innocence I turned round, only to see him in an elegance of undress and in a pose so like the sculpture as to cause me shock.

"The Marquis de Connaissance," I heard in an overtone, the stark magnetism of which drew closed the gold-laced alcove curtain separating us from the rest of the museum.

No sooner had he announced himself than the whimsy of fragrant light embalmed the entire room and my own rose eminence fructifyingly trembled in the virile fluctuations of air which fluted at my neck and fluttered the breast line of my blouse. In my most private parts I was sensationally warmed, and everywhere where contact urgencies pulse, there was titanic tingling.

"Who?" Was it whispered! Was it murmured! Was it only imagined!

"Arrangements must be made!"

Intuitively I understood the aggressive subtlety of His proposal and the damnable cleverness of His Disguise, and yet, still complicated by my own multiple involvements, I sought the certainty of a look back at the display case, hoping to elicit some explanation, some confession, some authority of consent.

The light in the case blinded me! And I was forced to turn again to the immensity of the Image now close to me, hugely blurring Its own outline till It was only an indiscriminate whiteness resisting denial. The Whiteness enveloped and inundated me, and, as if increased by Its own propulsive energies, expanded space to accommodate Itself. No longer was the cul-de-sac a cul-de-sac, but rather a cosmos of intoxication rendering orgasm.

Being done, the next thing I remember is an alarm going off in the museum, loud and irresolute, as if asking how! who! when! where! why! The cul-de-sac lost its aura of divinity, and I was aware that I was lying on the floor, Georgette and three guards standing over me, trying to snap me into uttering answers to their questions.

Over and over again I said I didn't know. I said something had been, but that it no longer was! I spoke of fulminating light and extremities of urgencies, of capitulation and resolution, and none of them, poor mortals that they were, understood! Georgette wept that she should not have left me alone, that I had just recovered from a very difficult time and that most probably I had anew been overcome by whatever it was that had affected me. She pleaded with the guards to carry me to a resting place where I might regain my senses in calm. But they were adamant; I could not be removed until it was determined what, if anything, I had to do with the missing Zeus.

For certainly the Zeus was missing and so was the Marquis de Connaissance. However, upon mention of his name, the guards seemed immediately relieved. For the Marquis was none other than the principal patron of their Museum, and, although none of them had seen him enter or leave, he was known to have mysterious ways, and it made perfect sense to them that he had decided to borrow back his loaned Zeus and had simply removed it from its case rather than go through the formalities. And then, looking at one another in a brotherhood of envious camaraderie, they helped me up, explaining that they quite understood everything now, for the Marquis was a man who took his pleasures where and when they presented themselves. With many apologies for their slightest doubting of my story, they ushered Georgette and me into the most *intime* of sitting rooms, and, serving us sherry and sorbet, prevailed upon us, when next we saw the Marquis, for they were sure we would hear from him again, to put in a good word for them.

I was, however, to hear from Zeus before I was to be attended by the Marquis. Hera, as usual infuriated with her husband's peripatetic affairs, and, without pausing to be original in her punishment, took vengeance on the object of his affections by striking me blind. And, of course, Zeus, refining his counter move with the ancient seer, Teiresias, compensated by giving me second sight into all but my own future.

It is, however, no easy matter having second sight without primary focusing faculties. Wandering all the time in a secondary world of before and after, events transposing and interposing themselves without stopping for breath at their meeting, one has no sense of anything actually happening. I was, in fact, being thrown backwards and forwards in time with tantalizing repercussions — beginning to do things only to find they had already been completed and believing some things accomplished before they had been begun. A juxtapositioning of events loosed from cause-effect/start-end syndromes.

As might be expected, this rattling of time resulted in a gibberish texture of language. And so the cryptic quality of the prophecies of ancient seers! and the great difficulty I had now in making myself understood. Georgette and I had literally to develop a language of our own. Finding my way tediously through my own memories, which were constantly being jammed by events of the largest historical past and the most diminished remoteness of the future, I eventually located the eleven word vocabulary used by Aunt Carole and Samuel Kitchelpop! Refining it and tagging in here-a-word, there-a-word of French argot, I was able to communicate adequately, if somewhat eruptively.

But enough to put out a shingle which daringly boasted: "MADEMOISELLE ROSE — FLORIST OF DESTINY: Bring me the Secret Blossoms of Your Heart, and I will Arrange the Bouquets of your life." The exquisite floriated patterns of light from the window of the little museum had inspired me, and with Georgette as my eyes, in an afternoon we converted our rooms into a veritable papier-mâché Garden of Eden. We scented the air, fashioned gowns for ourselves which petaled our necks, leafed our wrists and girdled our torsi like stems. And at the same twilight-of-the-gods that we had entered the museum, we crowned our heads with wreaths of laurel.

As if word of our enterprise had been spread by Mercury, within days, we flourished. The best of Paris society found their way to our door; we became an event at soirées, one of the most gleaming being at the home of the Marquis de Connaissance himself, who, having been thrown into a deep sleep by Zeus during the hour that the God was using him, sought our counsel in locating the missing sculpture which, of course, he had obviously not borrowed back. Upon being informed of the true train of events, the Marquis was so flattered by the use to which his externals had been put and by the fact that his prize objet d'art probably rested now on a shelf somewhere at the divine source of its inspiration that he felt Zeus had certainly designated him my protector, and he insisted that Georgette and I come to live in his house.

It was while we were gathering our belongings for packing that Georgette let out a cry which I could hear sounding in all the time aggregates through which I was constantly wandering.

"Ma chérie, the leetle bag! Eet ees gone! The leetle bag zat I found clutched in youaire fingers! I cannot find eet! I have used to keep eet heaire! But now eet eez not heaire! Eet has disparu!"

She cried on and on, asking me to forgive her, telling me again and again she had put it carefully among her most precious possessions, that she realized it had great significance for me, and she would not ever have been careless with it. She took my hand and placed it in the drawer where she had kept the bag, and she made me finger my way through the emptiness. As I did so, I was stabbed sharply by the knifing knowledge that the loss was not Georgette's, but that there were operatives of far greater import involved and that before I would know what they were I would have to stumble through the most awful rites of passage.

CHAPTER TWELVE
That It Should Come To This!

The stumbling began at the residence of the Marquis de Connaissance whose doors were open to the intellectual elite of the world. Artists, scientists, musicians, diplomats, philosophers — all and sundry of them had the run of the house. And run through it they did — around the clock and in shifts they sped, grunting and groaning, yeaing and naying the options which their real and intuited fervors afforded them. Agonies and ecstasies churned the blood! and paint and scribblings, layered on the walls, expressed the unstylized indulgences of their alternating physiological and emotional currents. In heavier times, they would sit, large numbers of them in small dark basement coves, even more darkly so as to be unable to identify each other, their very anonymity enhancing their sense of undemanding fellowship, every sigh, laugh, or growl freighted with understandings of the coexistence of their beings. And there and in such manner, each fellow would wrest from his heart his own *apologia pro vita sua*, long subterranean tales (so befitting the underworld ambience) which hushed even the silence of their wombs remembered.

With our arrival, Georgette and I became the hub of much of the activity. Overnight, utilizing the services of armies of workers, the Marquis built us a ravishing temple, a contemporary reminiscence of Apollo's at Delphi, setting it pristinely in his courtyard, itself a restoration of an Arcadian grove. There we held consultations, each of the petitioners baring his desires to us, pleading with us to see in the insubstantial light of the future some glint of his own enduring glimmer. Will I persist! Will I have resonance! Will I splatter the surface of mankind's muddling with the indelible residue of the deep waters of my spirit, my mind, my exalted soul! Some few were sent from our presence on wings of holy affirmation while others drew swords, guns, vials of poison and did away with themselves on the spot.

For his part, the Marquis had never been happier. Hedonist that he was, he gave little thought to his own immortality, but chose rather to entertain himself with the desperate concern his entourage had for theirs. He took bets on the prophecies, engaging in the most insensitive haggling for odds. Soon he was contracting himself as agent, manager, patron for those whom the gods had blessed, while at the great Janus-faced doors leading from the temple, he set up a discreet display of priceless antique weapons in the event the more unfortunate supplicant had come unprepared for the making of his own quietus and decided on impulse to rent or purchase the means thereof, the latter transaction carrying with it a guarantee for the buyer that although he himself might not achieve immortality, being buried with a weapon of certified distinction, would assure him of at least a footnote notoriety by association.

My rise to power brought me my share of enemies. There were those who accused me of being fraudulent, of deliberately concocting predictions of disaster in instances where I held a grudge for the petitioner or of my being in cahoots with the Marquis and making dire predictions for those whom he no longer held in favor. There were still others who would have been content to spend the rest of their lives smoking their pipe dreams and who resented me because they now felt themselves egged on by their peers to face up and get "the word" from the horse's mouth. Whatever — Georgette and I found ourselves increasingly threatened by such gross scare tactics as the old throw-the-dead-dog-into-the-room or the Gaelic refinement — a shrouded parrot by our bedside squawking, "Let them eat cake! Let them eat cake!" Our complaints to the Marquis brought his righteous indignation, and he proposed a seance in which a representative from the spirit world might be prevailed upon to authenticate my legitimacy to those of little faith.

At first I opposed the plan, for although I had grown accustomed to roaming in worlds past and future, I felt myself unskilled in establishing other-world contacts, and I was frankly concerned as to whom my gropings might lead me to run into. However, the excitement of the venture inspired the Marquis with firm resolution, and selecting that magic twilight hour, he arranged for the clan to gather. We had scarcely dimmed the lights and joined hands when into my second sight came a slowly materializing shape.

"I am Lucia of the cracked face and broken body, smashed by your father in days of yore and restored lovingly by you."

"Dear God!" escaped from my lips, causing all those gathered about me to lean forward in an attempt to hear what I was hearing.

"I was only a doll then, but I was your first love. Even more than that. My face of smithereens into which you slipped the last sliver of chipped lip engendered in you an enduring passion for the dismantled and dismayed. I have taken note, Gregory (How sweetly she called me by my rightful name despite the great distance I had come from myself!) and through the years I have waited in your world of hidden memories for the time when I could repay your great kindness and love. And now Zeus, who bids me apologize to you for all the problems he has caused you, has summoned me, idealized love that I am, to lead you through the trials still before you. For they are yea and many!"

I felt a tremble of exaltation from the others with whose hands I was still joined, and as if my darkness had been touched by Divinity, I could see the beautiful smiles that had settled on all their faces. I wondered if they were hearing what Lucia was telling me.

"Have no fears," spoke Lucia comfortingly to me. "They do not hear our conversations. Rather they are affected by the mesmerizing music of my siren voice, the sound of which recalls to each of them some lost love. For the voice of true love speaks to each his own." She sighed wide and long. "By the time we have done, there will be in each of their hearts a fullness of gladness or a fullness of sadness according to the terms that each has come to with his love, and this gladness or sadness will dissolve all doubts about you. For love, be it lost or found, conquers all, doesn't it Gregory!"

"So I have been told," I answered cautiously.

"You must throw caution to the winds," Lucia counseled, the music of her voice losing some of its melody. "You are about to play for keeps and the stakes are high! Why, Zeus and Hera have been raging at each other about you! You are a cause célèbre among the gods. No longer can you afford the wishy-washy mortal misgivings! You must be made of sterner stuff! I have been given instructions to give you full reign!"

"But I am not myself," I said, soulfully indicating a gesture towards my pubic area. "Would that I were Gregory again! For what good is a glory that may come to me, mistaken as I am for me. A man must be his true self if he is to achieve himself. And now I am at a loss." Lest my first pubic indication had been missed, I laid my hand limply in my lap.

"Do not suppose I do not know to what you refer," Lucia answered with sardonic ease. That your assorted parts be restored to you is of great importance to me as well. For I have loved you, Gregory, for all these years.

And although I am for fictive purposes your idealized love, there are even realer passions that we are meant to satisfy. To whit: I have been instructed by Venus herself in the vaulting art of amorous play, and it is to our mutual pleasures that I would have you repossessed. Your penis, which is now in the safekeeping of the gods, must be your grail which you will reacquire as you pass through your trials, which grail will assure me my earthly joys and gain you your entry into the realm of the gods!"

As Lucia discussed these matters with me, the curve and texture of her song became unendurably seductive to the others; the benign smiles that had suffused their faces took on provocative to lurid intimations, and the hands, which had been joined, broke apart and began to fuss and fondle in manners both genteel and obscene. Only Georgette seemed untouched by these particular side effects of the seance, as if somehow she saw the shadows which future events were casting before them. The more Lucia and I talked, the more Georgette removed herself, until, in a plaintive outburst, she cried, "Lights! geeve me lights!"

"Wanton wretch!" screamed Lucia in Georgette's direction. "You will never succeed in separating us! You will be done with soon." Then she confided to me, "But until such time, she will have to be intercepted since she is a worthy adversary for your affections. I must not underestimate her nor her sponsor. For, as I am being impelled by Zeus, I believe Hera is instructing her, and if I can judge rightly, what an awful collision there will be!

Already the harlot has interfered with our short time together; novice that I am in earthly sojourns, I cannot yet sustain even the mildest resistance and I must, woebetide! be gone! But I will be back, Gregory! Have no fear! I will come back stronger and stronger, and soon I will be able to endure even the light!"

Now piercing my second sight with countless points of dazzle and separating into the shattered fragments of which she was composed, she dissolved, leaving the room in a chaos of sexual frustrations. There were calls for more of her music, longing, angry, panting cries for the Siren's Song! The Marquis himself wept, promising me anything if I would make it possible for him to hear the sound again. (I did, of course, transcribe *Lucia's Song,* but the first edition caused such havoc that, on orders of the Department of Public Health and Safety, all copies had to be destroyed. Only the Marquis secreted his copy in a vault where he would from time to time sequester himself and sit and hum the tune; gradually his need for the melody intensified; his visits to the vault became predictably longer and more frequent until ultimately he shut himself up in the vault and went sighing and singing his way to madness and death.)

Such is the paradigm of the rest of my life! The wild heath knows no such ends as mine! Goethe! You called for more light! I call incessantly for more darkness — until that full and final darkness cover me! But the gods will not be merciful! And I am wracked by antemortemic agonies! Haaaaalllllllooooooo! Haaaaaaalllllloooooooooo!

I cry to wind and rain! Haaaaallllllloooooooooo! I cry to lightning sundered skies! Haaaaaaaaaallllllllllloooooooo! I cry! Haaaaaaaaalllllllllooooooooo! But there is no answer! Not even is there Echo heard! I yowl and tear at empty air —I fall upon the ground and beat my fists till flesh bleeds and bone is sore exposed! but, as if the inviolate air were deaf and dumb or of a substance unresponsive, I feel not even the vibrations of my beseeching! Holy! Holy! Holy is the sufferer! Ignorant of the ways of the Divine! Divinely mad! Madly untouched by even the tiniest tinge of pity! Haaaalllllloooooooooooo! Hallllllllllooooooooo! Hear me! But nothing is willed! For whatever is, cannot be moved! It is insensate! It will not obliterate! It does not even deny! My pen drops, my heart falters, my breath goes short in erudite remission, unremitting in its nothingness! Nadir of absence! Untuned silence! Remonstrances are naught!

So much had been indicated by Lucia! The gods had instructed her to give me full reign! What did that mean! What would be! What could be mine! Where would I be going! When would I arrive! How would my male accouterments be restored! Would I indeed ever enjoy the delicious debauchery of the Goddess of Love! How was Georgette to suffer in her rivalry with Lucia! And what sorry batterings would I receive as buffer in the marital contretemps of Zeus and his angry wife! Questions were born of questions; and, hastily dismissing everyone, even prevailing upon Georgette to leave me in the afterglow of my trance, I sat alone by the scented altar fire and listened for the testimony of my prophetic birds! But they were silent! How much their silence should have told me! Even their erratic chitter-chatter-chitter-chatter with which they entertained themselves as they exchanged centuries of gossip could not be heard! Had I been able to see them, I know they would have been poised, sheltering their eyes with wings, separating themselves from the vision of what lay before me, bathed as it was in a corrosive emulsion of blood and tears! Oh, silent, silent birds! Had I but heeded the absence of your song! Had I not been listening with unlistening ear!

It was my listening ear that shook me back to my awareness. It picked up a baby's cry, more of a baby's lament, perhaps a baby's dirge might additionally describe the sound. But where in my presence could such a presence be! The Marquis forbade children in his house, and I had no ragged sense of being displaced; my orientation seemed well connected to my Temple surroundings. I did not recognize the cry as that of Andromache's child being thrown from a cliff, nor of a slaughtered Innocent, nor of Moses rocking in the waterweeds. The cry was closer, somewhere in the intimate air, closer even than around me. A moment of swoon, of blank, and my speculation jolted! The sound was coming from inside of me! At first I clung to the possibility that it might be a plaything of my imagination, shaped in the wilderness of my mind, but then I knew it originated from lower down and in the gut of my anatomy.

"MaaaMaaa! Maaaaaaa! Maaaaaa!" came the cry.

I clutched my stomach! What fantasy! What hallucination! What infant voice spoke from my spasming innards!

"You carry within you a child of Zeus! The light of my life was lit when you were enlarged by the Lord of All Things."

I looked down at my middle. As if it were possible to see into my entrails! To corroborate what I could not comprehend!

"Though still unformed, I am wise beyond my years, for knowledge of myself has preceded its own being. It is before I am, so I may know how yet to be. Unlike a mortal child, I am prepared for the completion of myself even before I am determined. Oh cruel knowledge undenied! absorbed and suffusing! Thy will be done even before its doing!"

Was I to be a mother! How and alarm!

"Recently conceived, I will be torn ultimately from you! Woe is me! Woe is me! I will not know the safety of a single nurturing womb. I will be moved from womb to womb! Transient fetus that I am! Tied and untied is the cord of my life! Woe is me! To suffer such erratic maternal influences even before I see the light of day! Woe! Woe! Woe is me! Conceived by a mother who might under other circumstances have been my father, then torn from her, and, in a web of deception upon which my very life depends, surreptitiously shifted from mother to mother interuterine! I am much afraid! Weak I know it is to weep! And yet at this point in my gestation, courage is withheld from me! I have scarce developed heart! Who is there to comfort me! MaaaaaaMaaaaa! MaaaaaaMaaaaaaa! Can I turn to you for help! When you are yourself so woe distressed! Forgive the child who weeps in you! But I am not to be restrained! Maaaaaaaaa! Maaaaaaaaa!"

I, of course, found the whole business unsettling. As if my tension had not been extreme enough, this urgent and incessant cry in my guts uncentered the centrifugal force within me, and I felt myself loosed and flying in parts.

"Maaaaa! Maaaaa! Maaaaaaa! Maaaaaaa!"

The sound scattered me! I was blown by its urgency! I tried desperately to hold on! to garner a maternal instinct and pull myself together! To turn into myself! But to have learned of my pregnancy was much to bear, and in so unorthodox a manner was an even greater trauma! And then to hear of the imminent excision of the embryo! I did not know that I could endure more! but endure I would and would and would!

"MaaaaaaaMaaaaaaaa! MaaaaaaaaaaMaaaaaaaaa!" the cry persisted.

"Child, please," I offered. "Child! Child! please!"

"MaaaaaaaaaaaMaaaaaaaaaaaaaaMaaaaaaaaaaaaa-Maaaaaaaaaaaa!"

"You are driving me to desperation," I answered. "I am inadequately sustained in all of this! As you yourself observed, I am constitutionally unable to survive! I was not meant to be a mother! If the truth be known, I was not meant to be a father either! It is all a wretched wrenching of alternatives."

But the MaaaaaaaMaaaaaaaMaaaaaaMaaaaaaa continued unabated and unexplored. It scratched and scraped, it bleated and bled, it sought and conquered every aspect of my mind and body in which I sought escape, driving me deeper and deeper into myself until I had exhausted all possibilities and went — oh ye gods above us! — even to where this unborn babe was, wobbling into its own unchartered landscape!

Can we, in truth! so internalize ourselves that we are thrust back to our beginnings! Is it possible for the anima to be driven so into the labyrinth of self as to be lost somewhere in its own origins! Up to this moment of my life I would have said no — although certainly I have always subscribed to the separateness of body and soul as the experiences I have related substantiate! But from this moment on, I was unable to deny such an escape, for I was now a presence suddenly without form, identifying with those same awarenesses as the new life within me, with those same awarenesses, indeed, which had impinged themselves upon me when, lying in my mother's womb (if you will recall) crushed by my father's weight, my mother had shifted her coital position. Indeed, my child's cry had insidiously driven me further and further into my own being until I was ultimately converted to my single cell conundrum of a self. And then — even beyond — to that Great Before.

In that dark velvet luminosity, I was greeted by souls departed and unborn — all rushing towards me, around

me and even into me and through me, giggling and
weeping and welcoming and rejecting, hooting and
tooting, jiggling and swiggling — assembling and disem-
bodying themselves and each other — exchanging and
returning limbs, organs and assorted contrivances —
shedding the maimed, the withered, or the overgrown —
reflecting on their images in the bank of eyes which
opened and closed as they raised and lowered themselves somewhat like stars. I did not attempt to whisper
a greeting, for no one spoke, nor were identifications
personal. It was the essence that was being recognized,
not the associations. In absentia we were relating to what
we had never known, to what had been willy-nilly
imposed upon our mortal coils and coiling mortality.
How, I ask myself, did I know the knowing of it! Or not
knowing, feel the feeling of it! Even as I recall these times
of space, my underpinnings give way — and I am loose
and limbless, signifying to my usually saturated self —
nothing! Indeed the happenings at Gilmartisa were only
intimations of this — the real thing! But I gasp to think
how miraculously close the Miniharathomas had come
to the very secret of life! Remember, I said to myself, for
it has been shown to you in all its extremities.

Then —

"Have no fear! Have no fear, Lucia's here! It is the
way of Zeus, who has spoken to you through His/your
child, that has brought you to this place. He has learned
that his wife has learned of His/your child, and He has
had to act with haste! But with wisdom! Since the infant

is barely formed, he could not chance removing it from you, so he has removed you from around it, reducing you to what you were before you were and so freeing the babe. But be assured, the babe is now safe and away, lolling in Euterpe's womb."

"But where am I?" some voice of me was heard to ask.

"On the Immense Pile — where no part of us knows what it is or where it belongs. But again, I say fear not. For as you have been pressed by the infant cry to the extremes of self, so I can lead you beyond the limits of which you have dreamed. I can lead you to the Top of the Mountain where you will hear eternal voices. The Muses and the gods will open their Hearts to you — the clouds will veil your utterances in shadows lit by the self-revealing sun and moon — the wind will wail and whisper the manifest of the Primordial Mind. You will hear the birth of laughter and the ultrafrequent signal of silent mourning — beginnings and endings will converge for you, and you will lift the dead weight of the middle even unto the Towers of their Own Resurrection. And this you will see and have and grasp. But alas! you will have to die before you can be born again!"

"It is all too hazardous," I whined. "I have suffered enough. I have been subject to enough indignity. All I want is my parts again, and I will seek my fortune in my own mortal way."

"There is no mortal way for one of your kind," Lucia reminded me. "And even if there were, you have gone too far to profit from it. The choice is no longer your own. You have stepped over the line. You have penetrated the Unknown. You cannot turn back without results so dire as to make the trembling you feel now no more than a winsome predilection."

"I have never been a thing of courage. I am no hero. My father was a mushroom and my mother an hysteric — !"

"Your heroics are recessive. The potential is there! Remember your leonine ancestry."

"But put to the test, I know I am a coward," I argued.

"That is your rat self speaking! Begging, pleading! And it is that rat that must sacrifice itself before you will be entitled to the blessings of the gods. For the gods do not bless cowards." Then, with a passion which I heard as real and not merely as a modus operandi, she went on. "Gregory, Gregory! I love you! I know what you were! And I know what you can be! Together we can conquer not only the Worldly World but also the Everlasting One! We can be King and Queen first of the Secular, then of the Divine! I can offer you not only an extravagant life on earth! But I can offer you a seat in Parnassus! yes! even in Olympus!"

"The Spirit may be willing," I answered, "but the Flesh is weak."

"We shall make amends for that. In such manner you will first have to find the Willing Flesh which is tempered in the Corporeal Fires."

"Is there no other way," I urged. "Must I always be

bittered and bettered!"

As if my answer were coming from the least estimations of my being, I felt myself shrinking from any memory of mortal shape, dwindling to the discrepant dimensions of my rodent cowardice, to the niggling proportions of my rodent doubts, to the baseness of my rodent motives. Skeleton reassembled itself; flesh remolded itself; heart, soul, and brain were askantly realigned. Before me I saw all my shimmering goals ever turning and returning in the maze of endless recriminations. I was, indeed, the least of myself, the rat blindly seeking the way out of the intricate framework of my insidious need to escape.

Deprived of words, gifted now with only a pathetic squeak, I struggled at minimal communication to which I received no reply. With both a backward and a forward glance, I saw how little we know of what we are or of what we may become: where in our weakness lies our potential or where in our potential weakness lies our strength! how strong weakness turns us on ourselves, hoisting us upon our own petards, causing us to wiggle in the wayward winds of irretractable irresolutions! And how from that angling aspect, we wildly undo our wills until wrenched now from under the surly cloud of contentious cumulus, we diagnose a new order for ourselves and stretching, stretching, stretching, touch our suns!

But I am ahead of my story. More immediately no sun was to shed its rays on me; rather I was to be assigned to life beneath the Immense Pile — indeed, there is an underside even to the bottom — in the sullen swamp of the Intrinsic Slime.

Who shall descend unto this Lowest Place! He who shall have failed to ascend to the Highest One! He who lacks muscle, whose belly is puffed up with the foul air of the loftily lost! Who puts himself before his holiest intentions! Who would grovel rather than gain! Whimper rather than withstand! He it is who will grimly know this gritty grime of the Intrinsic Slime, skittering on rat feet with tremulous haunches and sliding on!

It is a place which shuns memory. So rank and gross as to offend the innermost eye of even sightless ones! Full of rats and bats arresting the trespasser with trailing cries of "Remember Me!" But I did not choose to remember them! I could not bear to remember them! I wanted only to find some way, any way, dare I say My Way to Salvation.

Yet hold! For there was no rushing on! There was only the slippery drag down, down, down beneath the downness of all things, sideswiped by the madding crowd slithering in the Slime. And with each lowering — oh! stop my heart! Disengage my brain! Must I reanticipate! With each lowering, more entrenched was I, fastened by this Inchoate Glue, unable even to inch my inclination to move! Was I ever to be suspended thus! Was I ever to be held by my own unrealized intentions! Inhaling their decay! For of this was the Intrinsic Slime! Of this same decay! Of this and only this! Of this alone and this! Beyond belief! Beyond imagination! Beyond all thus and so! And so and so and so! And in these very words, in the ad infinitum which they imply is this forever of our delay!

"Brother Rat," the creatures spat at me in broken unison, some voiced in this unholy chorus of beeps and squeaks losing their will from the start. "Even to communicate is an effort here. Thus we speak together, drawing upon our combined energies. For so enervated are we with the weight of lost achievements that no single one of us could by himself complete the articulation of a single idea." (More voices lost, others regained.) "Indeed, we have no single idea alone; we can only telegraph fragments to each other which combine and recombine in the supreme sophistry of whispering down the lane. But alas! we are never certain of the end of what we want to say, or if, in truth, we will get to that end, or, if that end is not just some unrealized exaggeration of the beginning or even a recanting of the beginning!"

And then a pause! Immeasurable! picked up first by one, then by another! And in between each pick-up of the pause, a pause more awful, as if each pausing needed pause to elicit and withstand itself! or, more diabolically, as if each pause brought pause to bear upon itself! But the pause did not refresh the creatures! rather it robbed them of the little will they had so that soon they seemed divested of even the breath of pause, and everything was stopped!

Like them, I was now becoming immobile, mushed into my place in the Intrinsic Slime, sealed into my own slot. Once or twice I thought I heard the heaving which might signal a new effort to communicate with me, but it expired retroactively before it dared exhaust itself! Even now as I write, I struggle against the lassitude with which these memories infect me and hold the hand which holds the pen so that I may push it on!

Where you may ask was Lucia all this time! This same question engaged me! If I was capable of any thought, and it came only in the weakest static, it was where was Lucia! Had I lost contact with her? Was she still to lead me? How differently I might answer her challenge now! But resolution was immediately unhinged! So that upon asking myself the question, I could not think of how I had answered her! Or whom it was I had not answered! Or even what the question was I had been asked! The more I tried to think, the less I thought! As if the effort canceled out the goal! Know you now the curse of the Intrinsic Slime! The thing tried is by this same trying undone! As Penelope unwove her web, so the Forces which determined the balance of turmoil in the Intrinsic Slime outdid her! The weaving was unwoven as woof met warp.

With this realization came the precluding sense of ripe defeat which characterized the souls lost in the Intrinsic Slime! What was the use? What did it profit me? Trapped as I was by my own efforts, resisted by the Slime of my own unmaking! But in that same instant, a final desperate insight, which inspired me to turn my limitation into my prison key! Do not try! If the trying undoes the deed, perhaps the not trying will do it! And so it was! And so it is! And so it will ever be! The self-surrender hard sought by genius, the giving up the will, the making of the self a vessel to be filled with the fulminations of revelations! Noah and his Ark! Newton and his Apple! Otherwise all is Vanity — Vanity! Vanity! all is Vanity!

(In my monograph, *The Unsuccess of Trying with Precise Insight in the Reverse Process Thereof!* I discuss the Tryer Phenomenon, painstakingly detailing the Non-Trying which Succeeds and the Non-Trying Which Does Not Succeed. The massive scholarly evidence I bring to bear on the subject was, of course, edited out of the more popular version of the article, "Diddlers and Doers," reprinted in countless Digests and How-To magazines; but even the watered-down version is marked by a brazen lack of compromise.)

As I suspected, so it came to pass. By allowing myself to sublimate the Slime, my subjective energies surfaced. These, left to their wiles, at first only fluttered, their fibrillations apparent to me by the remotest twitching of my whiskered lips. But then my body temperature, which I had allowed to slip sub-zero, began to rise rapidly, and, none of it being wasted by an exercise of my own will, the heat was soon melting the Slime in which I was entrenched. At first it only trickled, trickle by trickle, close to my body and then it ran in rivulets of perspiration, soon puddling under me, deepening as the Slime converted itself into a malodorous pool, then into a river of corrupt waters in which I found myself struggling to prevent my drowning. Harder and harder I paddled, exhausting myself! panting! then, remembering again to surrender myself, I floated in the smelly swirl, spun round and round, succumbing to dizzying nausea, to inexorable vertigo until, with furious dispassion, I was discharged into a swift current which emptied into — Oh! ye Sinners who would be Saints! — the Foulest flow of the sewers of Paris!

Heaven and Earth, I swore! It is not worth it! It is not worth love, nor fame, nor high fortune, nor yet a place among the Olympians! I will give up! I will die the cowardly death of a drowning rat if need be! I will not seek further for the Willing Flesh! I will expire this instant rather than inhale another breath of this Stygian putrescence.

But now above the slapping of the sewage slopping into me and the traffic noises of the streets under which I was being swept along, I heard Lucia's voice.

"Be of good cheer! Do not lose faith! Though you may think otherwise, you are doing well! Zeus is pleased! Behold a sign is being given unto you!"

And before me, raised on high, like the MENE MENE, TEKEL UPHARSIN on the Great Belshazzar's Wall, was an arrow shaped like my penis! radiating an iridescence whose pulsations violated indiscretion, sounding a trumpet call so blasting as to confound the simple and articulate the wise! Upward, Upward it pointed! And ever up and up, finally with a magnificent thrust urging itself into a narrow conduit! Not allowing myself to dwell on the harrowing associations of the imagery, I followed obediently, sliding and slipping, flooded from time to time by falls of atrocious waters. There are moments! thanks abounding! when the mind delivers itself from anything but the task at hand! All energies converge to make mighty the meek and to drive the heart and sinew with overtaking! So it is that heroes are born! And Jacks climb beanstalks!

But now what a rush!

What a swish! What a swash! What a swoosh!

What a splish! What a splash! What a spray sent me tobogganing around the sides of a bowl and flipped me over the rim onto dry floorboards! I huddled cornered in the darkness of this washroom, shivering from the cold and the wet and the eruptive procedures that had attended my sojourn! If I could rest, lie down and rest, collapse, sleep even at this station of my suffering! My brain sounded with such cliché aphorisms as "No rest for the weary," "We have miles more to go!" "Excelsior!" But a sudden letting-out of tensions allowed me only to shudder and weep, to weep for the release of the weeping! No tears of joy, no tears of achievement, no tears of majesty — no tears even for the sordidness of the travail — only the tears of spent energy, spilling from my eyes and washing from my face the awfulness of its encrusted debris.

My preoccupation with myself was now disrupted as from the next room, I heard sobbing even more violent than my own, unrestrained, convulsive, tearing away from itself on shriek waves. I thought I recognized the timber of the voice, and I skittered closer to the door, when, instantly, I was assured not only that my identification had been correct, but that I had, moreover, arrived back to where I had started my Parisian adventure, in the living/business quarters of Georgette.

"Ma Rose," she was anguishing, "she has just come to me and then she leave, disparu — Mais pourquoi! I come back to zee Temple, and she eez gone! I come back to my room and she eez gone! Nowhaire can I find her! Nowhaire ees she being! I make her my seestaire! And now I ave her no more! Ma chére Rose — she undairstand so much! She know so much! She daire so much!"

Her sobbing choked her words, and she reached across the bed, picking up a pistol from the bundle of rumpled sheets and blankets.

"What ees my life worth to me eef I ave not my Rose! She eez the perfume, she eez the flowaire of my innocence. She take my soul en her hand, and she geeve eet bourgeoning! She make me dance and sing and laugh!" Here Georgette tried to laugh, but the laughter surfaced into sobs and her fingers clenched tighter around the pistol, the barrel of which she rubbed against her cheek to wipe away the tears. "Zee pistol from zee Temple eez now my life — for death eez now my life — and zee one bullet waiting, waiting in zee chambaire of zee gun will I, enfin! make to enter zee chambaire of my heart!"

I, watching her minutely from my crouching place against the baseboards, now saw above her head, its arrow thrust powerfully sustained, my floating direction finder. What was it telling me to do as it spun in unreasoning reversals of itself. In answer I heard, like the luring obligato to Georgette's rending resolutions, new verses of Lucia's song:

If it were up to me
a dead girl she would be
I'd let her bullet hit her heart
and from herself let her depart
to leave us free.
But such is not to be! No, it is not to be.

Zeus wants the rat in you to die
her bullet's sure bull's eye
but gunshot blast will He resolve with penis
                                                        recoil
and antidote your dying flow of blood with your
                                              own semen fertile
to fashion from your life's liquors and His
                                              Godsome breath
a true rebirth where'er there should be death.

"Is there no mercy?" I managed to convey with the strongest squeak I could summon.

I saw the arrow limpen; and then, understanding that its reversals had been signaling me to take Georgette's place and die like a man by the bullet, I was assailed with outrageous doubt. (Ever the handmaiden of barrier bursting!) Was this representation really of my own sacred member! Was the sign legitimately my own! Was I being led up my own path! Or was I being led astray! I looked more closely at the floating penis, searching for some mark of recognition, some distinguishing I am yours! and only then did I realize how unobservant I had been all my life, taking myself so for granted that I could not even identify the darling parts of myself! Never I vowed would I again allow this complacency to invade me! rather once reborn, I would wallow in the compulsive accumulation of indelible detail — all manner of bits, pieces, nuts and bolts, flora and fauna! Ever the imperative for the artist!

As if my decision was being rewarded, I remembered now the guilty childhood synapse I had made between my limp penis and death on that illicit afternoon when, as a boy taking my pleasures, I had lied to my mother about applauding the genius of Socrates (see page 25). Indeed, from that afternoon on, the life-giving force had for me always been allied with death. So why not now! When it was veritably giving substance to my childhood fears in its undeniable injunction that I somehow take Georgette's place and sacrifice myself as a rat to death! When its limpness was again a reprimand! Here was my confirmation fatefully and philosophically confirmed! The penis was my own! The sign was mine!

Affirmation! Indisputable! Grail it was! as the iridescence with which the sign had originally announced itself now shone more blatantly and all afire! Which fire intensified! glowing with a tantalizing mystic fervor, till the radiating heat infused my rodent being with a manly urging of such stimulation that I felt I should implode. This urging flamed others within me, and they others till I was all arousals! Hot! Hot! Hot! I was! The Corporeal Fires, for that is certainly what they were, burning with a howling serpentine wind, pricking me blandishingly with pointillist dementia! When I felt I could bear the stimuli no longer! when all doubts had been incinerated by a crazed Willingness of the Flesh, I at last heard the Inner Self of All Selves cry out: ADVANCE! And what I knew to be Lucia's hand (I recognized the infinitesimal scars of finger cracks) pulled on that sign of manhood and I! Wild! wild! wild! with yes! yes! yes! scampered into the middle of the room in full view of Georgette who, upon seeing me, screamed AAAAAAHHHHHHHHH Rat! her body stiffening and shuddering, her hands flying into the air, the pistol swerving in its aim from her heart to mine.

"What profiteth it a man if he haveth his soul but remaineth a rat!" I heard the Olympians exult!

Lucia's song rose in confirming crescendo!

Georgette's AAAAAAAAAAHHHHHHHHHHH Rat! soared in dissonant harmonics!

BANG! went the pistol!

I felt the bullet blow me to bits, I felt my blood drain, but I felt at once also that arrow becoming my flesh, recoiling and releasing over me all of its flow!

By these miracles was I, from my own self, truly reborn, and by Lucia's hand still clutching, clutching, clutching what was transportingly my own, was I drawn on . . .

. . . to spurn faith, scorn death, and bear my hopes 'bove wisdom, grace, and fear . . .

CHAPTER THIRTEEN
Success is Short and
Not So Sweet as Roses

How swift! How short! How unchartered is success!
How full of enigmas! Bestowed by the gods, how subject
to their whims! They choose, they promote, they deprive!
They invert, subvert, deny and reverse our hopes and
graspings! Oh, Sisyphus! Sisyphus! All is pushing the
stone! Nor can one hope to read between the lines!

Indeed, Lucia's promise was fulfilled, but with such
éclat, such sumptuous unrestraint that, like some fire-
works display, it exhausted itself while still lavishing in
its pyrotechnical glosh! So complete and bountiful, yet so
instantaneous in its onset and detonative in its conclusion
that I am tempted to imagine that the whole extravagance
was indeed only a phantasmagoria evoked by her. From
the moment of the flash of gunfire and the evisceration of
my rat self (and correspondingly by virtue of my pre-
pregnancy incarnation, my rose self — although in my
success I still retained the sweet smell thereof!) through
my reincarnation and my sojourn in the Parnassian
realms and the indulgent cascade of accolade replete
with all the fringe benefits heaped by renown — from
that time till now seems like less than any measure of

time for it passed with the compression of a dream and with that absence of tenure that is the stuff of dreams.

To detail success carries with it the taint of boasting, though the way was not even mine. Rather the gods used me to convey aspects of their divinity — the books, the poetry, the plays, the sublime esoterica and the *Gilmartisian Oratorio* poured through me and reached the presses, the theatre, the concert stages as if by some beneficent wafting of an Olympian wand. The critics too were divinely inspired in my behalf, for their notices carried comments which only the gods might use to praise themselves. Nor did the public fail to hail me. I traveled to all the capitals of the world and to some of the remotest corners of the world. I was entertained by kings, queens, emperors, and chieftains. I was housed in palaces and hidden in monasteries, even spending three nights in the Sacred Grove of the Lorelei. I was loved (in the carnal manner) by women I had heretofore only seen in the most romantically illustrated novels, pamphlets, advertising materials and pornography magazines. I was sought after, quoted and imitated till on one occasion, at a gala, I was introduced to myself. And then, having come full circle, down I came as up I'd gone!

How, you are asking! How, you are wondering! What was the shattering event! How intricate the process! Was it a disastrous miracle like the Great Flood or the Plagues or the Ingestion by the Whale! So might it be compared, although its wellsprings were far simpler, far more within the compass of everyman's purview. It sprang from such mundane matters (had Lucia not so anticipated) as love and jealousy! Does this strike you as unimaginative that so luminous a star should be ripped from its constellation by such commonplace traducements! How often I remind myself that the moon shines only because it reflects the light of the sun!

But enough of the generalities! It is the specifics that will lacerate you! That will give you pause! That will cause you to plunge yourself into the grist of introspection! That will make you comprehend, as you have never comprehended, that even Zeus can be bested, that even he can be undone by a crisis wherein the matter does not try the cause, that Hell hath no fury like a goddess scorned nor earth no sadness like a woman's unrequited love!

Lucia enjoyed me! Both in the bedding and the heading sense! She stood beside me, behind me, at times even in front of me — consonant with the direction of the spotlight focus! She became my other self as she received my guests, fingered my medals and parchments, acknowledged my applause, completed my sentences, touched my verses with sighs and manipulated my inventions by alterations inspired by her in-house insights. She even delighted in procuring lovers for me — or, if the truth must out, she was compelled to do so by Zeus who, from his sacred grandstand, demanded some earthly pleasures also; for I am fairly certain that only my lovemaking to Lucia was my own doing; that the others were enjoyed simultaneously by Zeus who, by that same jimjackery he had used with the Marquis, inserted himself through my mechanism — but, if the gods will have no mercy on me, I shall have some mercy on myself and go no further into detailing this humiliation. Sufficient to say that Lucia, Zeus and I were completely entangled — enjoying what the other doled out — or what could be shamelessly doggy-bagged from the sumptuous feast!

Your breath is quickening! You are trying to sort the puzzle pieces! Well, let me speed the story as its disaster was speeded for me, like some filmed tragedy which turns ludicrous as the projectionist revs the action. Georgette's killing of the rat in the midst of her determination to kill herself rendered her *non compos mentis*. As a result, her concerns about her lost Rose were intensified and, enhanced by her sense of guilt, she was plagued with two possible explanations for Rose's disappearance, and sometimes, obsessively inspired by Hera, with a fiendish combination of both of them: One, that I (Rose) had become feverishly hallucinatory after the seance and, having wandered dangerously out on my own, had come to no good end; and two, that the gentleman whose organ she believed I had torn off had indeed been the one to steal it back from our apartment, and, having tracked us down chez Marquis, had kidnapped me when Georgette had left me alone in the Temple and carried me off to have his revenge. And so Georgette's recriminations drove her to the verge as she wandered through the streets of Paris in her continual searching for her Rose! Her lost sister! Given to her so mysteriously, and so mysteriously taken away!

Then Hera, playing on my penchant for the disfigured of womankind, led Georgette into my path one night as I swept from the stage door to my waiting limousine, inspiring her to cry out, "Rose! Rose! where eez my chère petite Rose!" and to slash her wrists, there on the spot, to which act I responded by scooping up the fainting figure, and, after getting her quickly for medical treatment, bringing her back to my apartment! This time, it was Georgette who opened her eyes to me after rescue (how blazingly ironic are the turns and twists of fate!) while I, staring down at her, whispered consolation to her: "You have been through a difficult time; you must rest, my precious one, and I will care for you!" Go back through these pages, dear reader! See! See! See! what a sexually inverted paraphrase this is of the very words Georgette had used to me when I had awakened in her quarters after she had found me lying in that rat infested garbage dump with my genitals clutched absurdly in a little bag! Inversions! Contraversions! Themes and Variations! Life is a fugue! Ill composed by some! Lacking any invention by most! Banal, even senile, as time makes rubato of it! But a fugue! a fugue! nonetheless!

As Georgette regained her strength, she called me her Prince des Ténèbres de l'Obscurité, for had I not rescued her from the physical night and the spiritual shadows which had enshrouded her. But then she would drift off again into melancholy and seek her Rose in the distraught memory of her semi-consciousness until, realizing I could not tell her the truth without making a raging lunatic of her, I fabricated an insouciance!

I told her that I knew Rose was safe — that, vraiment! it had been necessary for Rose to disguise herself and to seek refuge in a convent, for, as Georgette had suspected when she had found Rose in the dump and as Rose had attempted to deny, there roamed the streets a mutilated man bent on revenge. I told Georgette that Rose had asked me to look after her, for Rose did love her truly and now prayed hourly for her. (How I hated myself for this last sacrilege! I even ran from the room and fell upon my knees so that I might justify my reprehensible fabrication.)

Georgette pleaded with me to take her to the convent where Rose dwelt or, if Rose wished her whereabouts to be a secret, to ask Rose to come to see her even once! But I told Georgette that Rose had vowed, as her penance for the terrible deed she had done, to see no one who might in any way be dragged into the intricate web of her crime and punishment. For was it not possible that the mutilated man, unable to take revenge on Rose herself, might take revenge on the dearest one that Rose loved. I even told her that in some marvelous way I was part of the secret of the heart that she, Georgette, had been sensitive enough not to probe as she had sat on the edge of the bed that night of her first dialogue with Rose! A gasp! a tear! a smile! a despair! Then a fright! I had overstepped my ingenuity. Into Georgette's eyes came the terror that bespoke the question: Was I, myself, the man of whom she should be afraid! Was I only being kind to her now to have the best of all possible revenge! I allayed her concern by gently exposing myself to her. She lost herself in my privates, kissing me over and over again in relief that I was not the villain, and in gratitude that I had saved her and been so loyal to her Rose. And beyond, she promised never to doubt me again; she promised undying faithfulness; she wept tears of comfort, joy, and love!

It was, of course, at this moment that Lucia entered the room, and mightily aroused was her rage. I tried to calm her, struggling to reveal to her and at the same time conceal from Georgette the twisted strands of an unutterably complex plot and counterplot. I even suggested that it was not I but Zeus who was enjoying the fondling and caresses of the distraught Georgette now drifting into a blissful doze.

Lucia remained unconvinced and suspicious while Georgette, all innocence, continued to be dazzled by the continuum of her new life. And although Lucia tried to keep Georgette in the background, she was fighting a losing battle, for Hera had conceived a plan which would undo us all and serve our remains to her mighty husband on a bloody platter of revenge.

Why, you may ask, did Zeus not put an early stop to what he himself must have known would be the outcome. Perhaps he was tiring of the unbridled revelry; perhaps he saw he had more to gain by letting his wife win this battle while he continued to win the larger wars; but I suspect that once he realized that he was being shafted, he became tacitly involved in this fandango. I suspect that he became himself a silent partner in bringing about his wife's revenge; to serve the greater cause — to run away today so he could fight another day. Or perhaps he did choose to remedy the situation, but the play intrigued him more than the plotting of it, and like the Miniharathomas, he left the action to his minions, who bungled it.

The inevitable happened. The more Georgette's love became apparent (her displays of it were now increasingly public), the more Lucia's jealousy grew. In fury after fury, Lucia would sit me down and call me to account, threatening all kinds of hanky-panky if I didn't get rid of Georgette. And what was the matter with me! Was I unwilling to save myself! Was I subconsciously so tired of the struggle that I gave it up even while believing I was carrying it on! Was I testing my waters to see how far I could bring myself! Was I challenging the gods! I don't know! I do know only that I told Lucia I was entitled to some life of my own, that I was feeling threadbare with serving her and the Olympians, and that if I was to be of any value to myself or even to our mutual divine strategies, I had to assert myself! Was it just childish perversity on my part! Or robust arrogance! Speculate for me, dear reader! I have reasoned and unreasoned till I feel madness would be a blessing!

In any event, Lucia raged, and I not only did not cast Georgette away, but I even increased my attentions to her. Some might say I was evincing a latent antagonism for my mother who had those many years ago given

Lucia to me and then, after my father had destroyed the doll, forced her will on me by making me reassemble Lucia. I have even given thought to having been taken over by my father's desire to annihilate me or by the dead sister whom Lucia had replaced. Whatever the forces driving me to this behavior, Lucia was determined to meet their ingenuity. She attempted all sorts of mean tricks, even pretending to befriend Georgette, and then, showing her the tiny cracks in her own skin, informing her of how she might disfigure herself to make herself more attractive to me. From such subterfuge, she sidled little by little to the cliff edge of murder.

It was the night of the gala premiere of the *Gilmartisian Oratorio*! How inaccurate that the end should come at the moment of such transcendence. The performance wafted and resounded, deliquesced and opalesqued, thundered and intimidated — as if Sung by Hosts on High accompanied by the Forces of Nature Themselves. The audience, unable to bear the intensity of exposure to such raw impulses, merged with one another to seek some holding ground, melting and smelting into one another, scorched by the white heat of the Nakedness of Inspiration and Execution! If all had not been bathed in Divinity, the concert hall would have appeared a battlefield, so diagonally were limbs embraced, so guttural were whispers and gasps, so agonized was the transfiguration on faces. If with my first play I had torn audiences asunder, I had now, at this ultimate moment of my career, fused them!

The last notes — oh! scarcely notes, scarcely even tones, rather aural emanations from the Muses themselves — were dissolved, leaving the world in resurrected harmony, when — Sacrebleu! — it was as if Hell had conquered Paradise! Wracked by the ecstasy of the moment, the jealousy in Lucia went berserk, and she attacked Georgette who had been adoringly involved with me! But she attacked her in no mortal way! Yea! Nay! What then did she do! Oh, ye gods! give me strength to bear witness!

She consumed her! Consumed! What means consumed, you demand! How does one consume another! How does one mortal shape, even if engendered by Divine Madness, consume! I say, Enlarge your Imagination! Break through those barriers of preconception! Redefine limits! And You will Understand! You will Fathom! You will Envision and then You will put out your Own Eyes!

Oh, Medea! Surely you were present! Surely you were unearthed, called upon by the Enraged Hera to Inspire! Surely it was you who so Perverted the Purity of the Hour as to cause it by contrast to augment Lucia's mania, to make it grow and grow and grow — until Lucia, unable to breathe of it gasped for Air — her Eyes Widening and Widening into one Huge Opening through which the Green-Eyed Monster within her reared its Ugly Head and rapaciously consumed one by one every feature, every shapely aspect of its Nemesis, leaving only a blood-green luminosity where Georgette had sat!

The audience in the concert hall, slowly disentangling themselves from their rapturous involvements with the *Oratorio* and each other, cast their eyes up at the Grand Tier Box where Lucia, Georgette, and I had been sitting! And what they saw set them wild! Lucia, still unable to satisfy herself and puffing herself up beyond which even the most extreme extension of herself would allow, exploded like some expanding universe with a big bang, scattering fragments of herself and disgorging Georgette hither and yon! In one instant both of my women were, before the eyes of the world, reduced to the smitherins my father's act had foreshadowed! while I, losing the Divinity I had gained in my travails and reverting to my former dichotomized confection, stood in a quandary, my rose self transfixed in the resounding echoes of my *Oratorio*, my rat self sniffing the already putrefying remains about me.

How could anyone be expected to supply even an irrational explanation for the cause of these events; how could any wild crowd, officers of justice, lawyers, juries, heads of state, who might have intervened on my behalf, be expected to accept so inadequate an answer as my tale of truth. And so I was held responsible, and concerned citizens divided themselves into two camps, both of which considered me guilty, but each of which accounted with different reasons for what was designated as my depraved crime. There were those who maintained I was mad and those who maintained I was diabolically inspired. And in each camp my adoring public, unable to desert me in my hour of need, found salvaging and assuring justifications. In the camp where I was deemed mad, my madness was attributed to my mortal inability to control the divine furies which inspired me and drove me to create with such bravura! In the camp which declared me diabolically inspired to the heinous acts, the consensus was that the gods now demanded where they had previously bestowed! Be all that as it may, I was apprehended and thrown into the nearest dungeon — and lest the judgment of malefaction not cover the consequences, I was further straitjacketed to encompass the diagnosis of insanity.

Can you believe that after all these things, the gods could devise even more cruel irony! Can you believe that even they could forge still another two-edged sword! If you say no, you have not experienced the ways of the Divine. For rather than have done with me, they have managed to free my hands when my guards turn their backs and to put into my fingers the crepuscular instrument of writing with which I record this history so that I may despair after I revel , cringe after I exult — indeed, so that I may, like some bound Prometheus recall my grandeur even while I endure the daily devouring of my liver!

But now — I cry out! I say to you — Prometheus suffered because he had defied the gods! I did not defy them! They gave me the fire! And I, every moment and at every crossing of my life, left myself open to their intricate assortment of wayward rewards and wizening punishments! I have been their servant! I have been their messenger! Why then have I suffered so! Why then! Because, I am forced to conclude, I am, for all purposes, the very embodiment of their whimsy — and my dual nature is their declaration of themselves, as is this chronicle written while I await whatever end they have in mind for me and traversing in turns as it does the maze of a rat, and, redolent and redeeming, that of an erratic Roman de la Rose.

Arnold Rabin spent the early years of his professional life as a network TV writer-director-producer, also serving as Chief of English Language Television Services for the United Nations and as Administrator of Special Projects for Channel 13, the PBS station in New York. During these years his documentaries and TV plays received such commendations as a Harcourt-Brace Best TV Play Citation, a New York Emmy nomination, an Edinburgh Film Festival showing, and Ohio State and Variety awards.

He then left television to concentrate on his own writing projects. His short stories and essays have appeared in such commercial and literary quarterlies as the *Ladies' Home Journal, Journeymen, Changing Men, Chicago Review, Massachusetts Review, descant* and *Brushfire* and most recently a children's Golden Book. As a playwright, he was selected a Fellow to the Edward Albee Foundation, and he is the recipient of the Distinguished Play Award from the American Council for Theatre and Education, the Denver Drama Critics Circle Best New Play Award, and the Drama League of New York's Playwrights Award. He has received a playwriting grant from the New Jersey State Council on the Arts and a creative writing grant from the National Endowment for the Arts on which *The Rat and The Rose* was written.